Sugar Spinelli's
Little Instruction Book

I swear, if there ever were two people who deserved to get together, it's that nice Beth Cochran and that sinfully handsome Jarred McCoy.

Beth has more than she can handle with the twins, her son and that old wreck of a house. But I hear Jarred is just the fellow to step in and lend a hand. Something tells me, though, that Beth isn't the only one who needs help. McCoy looks to me as if he could use a healthy dose of a family's affection, a place to belong and, most of all, the love of a good woman. Now, let's just hope he's smart enough to see the gift he's been given....

Dear Reader,

We just knew you wouldn't want to miss the news event that has all of Wyoming abuzz! There's a herd of eligible bachelors on their way to Lightning Creek—and they're all for sale!

Cowboy, park ranger, rancher, P.I.—they all grew up at Lost Springs Ranch, and every one of these mavericks has his price, so long as the money's going to help keep Lost Springs afloat.

The auction is about to begin! Young and old, every woman in the state wants in on the action, so pony up some cash and join the fun. The man of your dreams might just be up for grabs!

Marsha Zinberg
Editorial Coordinator, HEART OF THE WEST

The $4.98 Daddy
Jo
Leigh

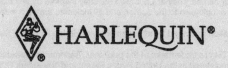

HARLEQUIN®

TORONTO • NEW YORK • LONDON
AMSTERDAM • PARIS • SYDNEY • HAMBURG
STOCKHOLM • ATHENS • TOKYO • MILAN • MADRID
PRAGUE • WARSAW • BUDAPEST • AUCKLAND

Jo Leigh is acknowledged as the author of this work.

ISBN 0-373-82598-6

THE $4.98 DADDY

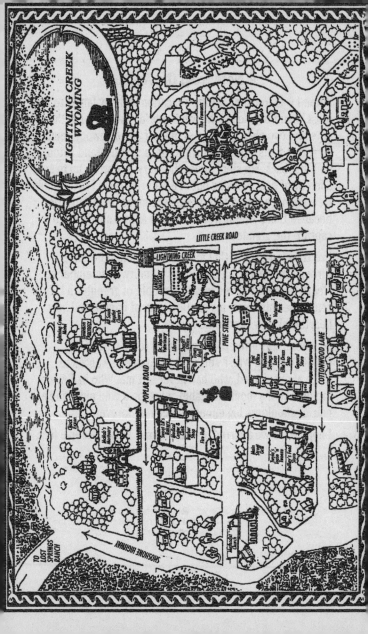

A Note from the Author

When I was fourteen, I took a vacation with my family to the most beautiful place in the whole world: Wyoming. For three days and two nights, my sister, myself and a cowboy named Jarred rode into the great wilderness of the Grand Tetons on horseback. We slept under the stars, and woke up to see a family of deer drinking out of a watering hole. I don't think we said more than a half dozen sentences the entire trip, because there simply weren't words expressive enough to capture the grandeur.

I've traveled back to that magical place and time often through the years, but only in my memory. I remember so clearly how kind Jarred was to a couple of greenhorn kids. I remember his voice, his gentle sense of humor, and how heartbreakingly handsome he was.

So when I was given the opportunity to be part of the HEART OF THE WEST series, it was Jarred I wanted to write about. Jarred, who had never left me. Who had made me dream of a mountain cabin, a fire on a cold night and a pair of shoulders big enough to lean on forever.

I hope you have a Jarred in your dreams. We all deserve that.

Jo Leigh

To Marsha Zinberg, for inviting me to the party.
Thank you.

CHAPTER ONE

THE DILEMMA WAS OBVIOUS. Go play on the jungle gym and risk running into that stinky toad Steven, or go to the arena and see what was happening in there. As usual, Debbi and Karen Cochran didn't have to argue about it. They both hated the stinky toad so much that seeing him would ruin their whole day.

Debbi eyed the boys playing in the big log fort. "Mom said we should stay here."

"But she's working in the kitchen," Karen reasoned, her gaze caught by the hubbub at the entrance to the outdoor arena.

"Caleb will tell," Debbi said.

"Only if he finds out."

The girls looked at each other and, in that way only identical twins understand, made up their minds in a flash. They grabbed hands and headed for the arena, not at all sure what they were going to find. Mommy had said that there was going to be an oxen. Debbi had seen a TV show where there was an oxen, which was a kind of big cow. They both liked cows.

They didn't run. There was too much happening to rush. Besides, all the grown-ups liked to smile at them. "I bet nobody smiles at the stinky toad," Karen said.

"Look over there." Debbi pointed with her free

hand to a group of grown-ups standing around a man with a camera. "That's for TV."

"How do you know?"

"Because I saw it on *Reading Rainbow*."

Karen nodded. *Reading Rainbow* was always right.

They moved closer to the TV man, hoping to see someone special, like Big Bird or Galaxy Man, but it was only some lady. With a simultaneous shake of their heads, they went back on course, the smell of barbecued hot dogs making their feet go faster and faster until they gave in and ran.

There were a whole bunch of tables set up, and people had paper plates full of ribs and hot dogs and hamburgers and potato salad and coleslaw and macaroni salad. Debbi liked hot dogs the most, and Karen liked spaghetti, but nobody had any spaghetti.

Debbi pulled her twin toward the hot dog grill, but then they saw Caleb and they ran toward the arena as fast as they could go. If their big brother caught them here, he'd tell Mom, and then she'd make them come inside because they couldn't be trusted.

Pushing their way through the crowd at the entrance, they made it, only to stop still to look around. It was a big circle, like at the circus, only without the top, with rows and rows of seats and a dirt floor, and then there was a big stage with chairs and some men sitting there. Some lady with a bunch of papers walked around talking to the men.

"The teacher," Karen said knowingly.

"Yeah."

"Where's the oxen?"

Debbi shrugged. "Maybe he comes out later."

They heard a squeal and then a voice, real loud, saying, "Ladies and gentlemen, please take your seats. The oxen is about to begin. Welcome to Lost Springs Ranch for Boys, and the first ever bachelor oxen. I can tell you all want to get things rolling, so, ladies, put your hands together for our first bachelor, Dr. Robert Carter.''

The clapping and hollering erupted with a blast, and Debbi and Karen looked at each other. ''What's a bachelor?'' Karen asked.

Debbi shrugged. ''Probably a cow doctor.''

They headed toward the big stage, figuring the oxen must be behind it. The guy was still speaking, all about some other guy and how he was a poet, but they didn't care about that. Not when there were oxen to find. They reached the side of the stage, where there were some more steps. Beyond them were a few cabins.

Quick as a wink, the girls headed for one of the cabins. Just as they did, a man came hurrying toward them. A really tall man.

Karen and Debbi both looked up as the man got closer. He stopped a little bit in front of them and smiled.

The girls stopped breathing. They looked at each other with wide eyes, then back at the man. It was *him*. They knew it instantly. For absolute sure. Even though he wasn't wearing his Galaxy Man cape or his bright blue shirt, they knew. This was better than oxen. Better than Big Bird. This was the best thing in the whole wide world.

''Excuse me, ladies,'' he said, his voice exactly like it was supposed to be. Better than Batman. Better than Superman.

He walked to the stairs and climbed them, and the girls just kept staring, wondering when he was going to take out his transformer ray and change into Galaxy Man. They didn't want to miss that for anything.

He stepped onto the stage and they couldn't see him anymore, so they raced back in front, only more people were there now so they had to squeeze through them to see the stage. There he was, sitting down next to the regular men. Debbi hopped from one foot to the other in her excitement. Karen just kept squeezing her hands together.

"What's he going to do?" Karen asked.

"I don't know. Probably ride the oxen. Or maybe he has to beat up some bad guys."

Karen nodded, her gaze riveted by her hero. He looked just the way he looked in the comic books. Taller than Mom by a lot. And even though Karen had only seen him in drawings, she'd always known that he really did have those big wide shoulders, and that his hair was wavy and dark. But the thing that made her absolutely sure he was Galaxy Man was that he had those light-blue eyes that could see through walls and stuff. He wasn't smiling now, and that meant he was on the lookout for evil. He probably had his ray gun in his jeans.

"What are they doing?" Debbi asked, jerking her head toward the man at the microphone, who was talking too fast.

"I don't know." Karen looked around for someone nice to ask, and she saw the teacher with the clipboard. She ducked under the arms of a cowboy, pulling Debbi along with her, until she could tug on the teacher's pants.

"Hello there," the lady said, smiling.

"What are they doing, miss?" Karen asked.

"Yeah, what are they doing?" Debbi repeated.

"This is a bachelor auction," the woman said. "It's for charity."

"Huh?" Debbi said.

"My goodness, you two look exactly alike. How does your mommy tell you apart?"

"I'm older," Karen said.

"I've got a Mona Lisa smile," Debbi added.

"I see." The woman leaned down so she didn't have to talk so loud. "A bachelor auction is where the women get to buy one of our nice men for a little while. Just for fun."

"Buy them?" Debbi asked, more confused than before.

"Yep."

"What do they buy them for?"

"Well, some of the ladies want the men to take them on dates."

"Do they hafta go?" Karen asked.

The lady nodded. "That's the deal."

"So where's the oxen?" Debbi asked.

The lady looked at her funny. "Oxen?"

Karen turned to her sister. "It's not a oxen. It's an auction," she said, pronouncing the word carefully. She turned back to the lady. "Right?"

"Right," the lady said, her grin bigger than ever.

Debbi frowned. "I don't get it."

"Okay," the lady said. "Let's say you had some money that you wanted to give to charity. Do you know what charity is?"

The girls nodded, remembering the money they put into the silver box at the grocery store.

"So you have this money, and you think one of the men on stage looks nice. You offer to buy him. If you offer the most money, then you win. You give the money to the charity, and then you get to have a date with the man.''

"Really?" Debbi asked. "I didn't know you could buy people.''

"You can't for real," the woman said. "But you can for charity.''

"Can anyone play?" Karen asked.

"Anyone with money.''

Karen nodded. "Thank you.'' Then she headed back to the front of the stage, pulling Debbi along with her.

Galaxy Man was still sitting on the last seat along with about five other men. They listened to the fast talker for a long time, but it wasn't that interesting. Some cowboy got sold, and a private detective, and a breeder. They all seemed like nice men, but they weren't *him*. When it was almost time for Galaxy Man to stand up, Debbi turned to Karen. "You think we could buy him?''

Karen nodded slowly. "Maybe. Do you have any money?''

The girls went into the pockets of their matching pink shorts and pulled out all their money. They'd spent a dollar just last night on the latest Galaxy Man comic, but they still had one dollar and six cents left.

Just as they finished counting their money, a shadow fell over them. An all-too-familiar shadow.

"All right, what are you two brats up to now?''

The girls turned to face their brother, Caleb. He was nine, and he was mean, and he was probably going to tell Mom that they'd left the playground. But the possibility of buying Galaxy Man was too great a temptation, and in that way only twins have, they decided to go for it.

"Do you have any money?" Karen asked.

Caleb frowned. "Why?"

"We need it," Debbi said. "It's a 'mergency."

"What kind of an emergency can two pip-squeaks like you have?"

"Caleb, come on. We'll do your chores for a week."

"A whole week," Karen reiterated, pleading in her most urgent way.

"I don't have any money," Caleb said, but he wasn't really paying attention to them any longer. He was listening to the fast talker.

"Jarred McCoy, one of our Bonus Bachelors, owns the McCoy Construction Company in Houston. Maybe some of you ladies have some cupboards that need fixing, eh?"

Everyone laughed except Caleb. The girls didn't understand his serious face. He was studying Galaxy Man real hard. Maybe he'd figured out who he was, too.

"Caleb, please!" Karen whined.

"Please, Caleb!" Debbi added, matching her sister's whine exactly.

He didn't look at them. He just kept watching Galaxy Man. And listening to the other man talk about how he could build anything, and how he was a handy man in more ways than one. Just when they were about to give up, Caleb reached into his pocket and pulled out some crumpled-up money. He handed it to Karen, then went back to watching.

As quick as they could, the girls counted the money. Altogether they had four dollars and ninety-eight cents. It was almost five dollars, and five dollars was more than they'd ever had.

The fast talker was going a mile a minute, pointing and speaking in his weird way. Debbi grabbed Karen's hand, and they raced to the steps, ducking and dodging grown-ups. Once they reached the stairs, no one blocked them, and they ran straight up to the stage. Debbi stopped as she looked at all the people in the stands. There were so many! Karen tugged at her hand, and they started walking toward Galaxy Man and the fast talker.

Debbi's heart beat so hard in her chest she could almost hear it. She wanted to quit and go back down, but then Karen would be mad.

Karen took one last good look at Galaxy Man, just to make sure, and then she pulled Debbi along with her until she reached the fast talker. She heard him say, "Going, going..." Then she tugged on his pants.

The man looked down. Galaxy Man looked down. Everything got real quiet.

"Hi there, little ladies. What can I do for you?"

Karen swallowed. "We'd like to buy him, please."

"You'd like to buy him?" the man said, but real loud into the microphone so everyone could hear. They all started laughing, but Karen wasn't going to run. Neither was Debbi. It was too important.

The girls nodded, then Debbi held out the money. "We have four dollars and ninety-eight cents," she said, in a real quiet voice.

"Four dollars and ninety-eight cents?" the man repeated.

Everyone laughed again, but a whole bunch of people went "Awww."

"I'm afraid the bid is a little low—"

"Wait," Galaxy Man said. He looked at the girls, his X ray eyes probably seeing right into their bones.

"I think that bid is real generous." Then he whispered something to the fast talker.

"Okay, then," the man said into the microphone. "Mr. McCoy is going to accept the bid for four dollars and ninety-eight cents, and he's going to make a personal donation to match the previous bid of two thousand dollars."

Everyone started clapping and hollering. Karen and Debbi turned around, startled at the noise, not understanding at all what was going on.

Then Galaxy Man crouched down and they forgot the crowd and the hollering. "I'm Jarred," he said. "And it looks like you girls just bought me."

"Jarred?" Debbi said, confused.

Karen leaned over and whispered, "He's in…um, in-incontinent. You know, pretending to be someone else."

"Oh," Debbi said, nodding.

"And who are you?"

"I'm Debbi Cochran."

"I'm Karen Cochran."

"How old are you, Debbi and Karen Cochran?"

"We're six," they said, both at the same time.

"Six? That's a good age. What do you say we pay the man, and then let's get off this stage to start our date."

The girls nodded, and Debbi handed the fast talker the money. He smiled again, and everyone clapped some more, but then the best thing happened. Galaxy Man took them both by the hand, and they walked to the stairs.

As they reached the ground again, they saw Caleb. He looked funny, like he'd swallowed a fly or something.

"That's Caleb," Karen said, pulling Galaxy Man toward their brother. "He's nine, and he's our big brother."

"Hey, Caleb," Galaxy Man said in his rough voice.

Caleb took one step back, but then he puffed up his chest. "Are you really a master builder?"

"Jarred McCoy," Galaxy Man said. "Master builder." He let go of Debbi's hand and held his out to Caleb, just like Caleb was a real grown-up.

Caleb shook his hand for a second, then stuffed both of his hands in his pockets.

"I'm guessing you three aren't here alone," Jarred said.

Caleb, Karen and Debbi all shook their heads.

"Who's with you? Your mom? Your dad?"

"Our dad lives in San Diego," Karen told him.

"Our mom is working in the kitchen," Debbi said.

Caleb didn't say anything.

Jarred nodded. "Caleb, how about you show us the way to your mom?"

Caleb shrugged, but he started walking away from the arena. As they passed through the huge crowd, people started clapping and making a clear path for the four of them, smiling and waving and acting downright goofy. Debbi and Karen just held tight to Galaxy Man's hands, and they didn't care about anything else. Galaxy Man, the greatest hero in the universe, belonged to *them!*

Once they left the arena, the cooking smells hit hard, and the girls spared a glance at the hot dog grill, but Caleb was walking so fast they didn't even get a good sniff. He led them past an old tree that had a blanket hanging from it, straight toward the big building where Mom worked.

Galaxy Man dropped their hands to open the door, then he waited until they were all inside. Caleb went first. Galaxy Man started walking, but this time he didn't take their hands. Debbi thought about grabbing him, but then Karen moved to her side and they just followed down the hall to a big white door.

As soon as Caleb pushed the door open, they heard the sounds of the kitchen. Running water, clinking glass and lots of people. They hurried behind Galaxy Man until they were inside, looking for Mom.

"There," Karen said, pointing toward a big sink, where their mom was washing dishes.

"That's your mother?" Galaxy Man asked.

"Yes, sir," the girls said at the same time.

"She works here at the ranch?"

"Only today," Caleb told him, heading toward her.

Karen and Debbi looked at each other, wondering what their mom was going to say. She'd probably be mad, but then they'd explain that it was for charity. She was real big on charity.

Caleb and Galaxy Man had almost reached the sink, so the girls hurried to catch up, nearly knocking over a stackful of plastic glasses. But they made it before Mom turned around. They stood on either side of their prize, so excited they thought they might burst.

Mom didn't notice them right away. She just wiped her bangs off her face with a soapy arm, then plunged her hands back in the water.

"Mom," Caleb said, real loud.

She turned so fast they all got sprayed with soapy

water. It hit the girls on the chest, but it got Caleb in the face. They couldn't help laughing.

Mom's eyes got wide when she saw Galaxy Man. She didn't say anything, though. She just wiped her hands on the ugly stained apron she had on and looked from Caleb to Karen to Debbi and then back to Galaxy Man.

"What's this?" she asked finally.

Karen and Debbi took one last brief look at each other, then grabbed Galaxy Man's hands. "Look who we bought, Mom," Karen said.

"Yeah, Mom," Debbi added. "Can we keep him?"

CHAPTER TWO

BETH FELT HER JAW SLACKEN as she studied the man in front of her. His height would have been daunting in and of itself, but coupled with his Rocky Balboa build, startling light-blue eyes and dark wavy hair, it left her completely unable to form a coherent sentence.

"Mom?" Debbi prodded.

"Can we?" Karen added.

Beth tore her gaze from the imposing stranger and focused on the girls. "Can you what?"

"Keep him?" Karen said, hope shining in her eyes as she practically jumped with anticipation.

"Keep him?" Beth repeated, trying to understand. "Why would we keep him?"

"Because we bought him," Karen said.

"At the auction," Debbi explained.

Beth's gaze shifted to the man, and she couldn't help but notice how far her head had to move back just to see his face. He must be at least six foot five. "I'm sorry," she said. "I don't understand."

He smiled, easing her disquiet as if by magic. "Maybe I can help," he said. "I'm Jarred McCoy. One of the bachelors. Your girls came up with the highest bid, so here I am."

"They came up with the highest bid?" she asked,

checking to make sure there weren't two other girls hiding behind him.

"Four dollars," Karen said.

"And ninety-eight cents!" her sister added.

Beth crossed her damp arms over her chest. "*That* was the highest bid?"

Jarred shook his head, causing a lock of dark hair to fall across his forehead. "Well, let's just say it was the most heartfelt bid."

Beth's gaze got stuck on the errant lock of hair. She had an overwhelming urge to brush it back into place. Which told her she was spending far too much time with her children and not enough with grown men.

At that thought, she brought her hand up to swipe her own hair back off her forehead, and then it dawned on her that she had soap on her hands and in her hair. With this dirty apron, she must look like something out of the gutter. She didn't have a lick of makeup on, and even the shoes she'd worn looked like something an elderly nurse would wear.

She took a step back, then realized she'd have to step all the way to California if she wanted him not to notice how bad she looked.

His smile faded and his eyes narrowed, perplexity making him impossibly more attractive. "Is everything all right?"

"What? Oh, sure. Yeah. Fine. No problem."

The grin came back, at least half of it did. Great, so now he thought she wasn't just the scrubwoman, but the insane scrubwoman.

"I didn't mean to make trouble," he said. "I just came out here to pay off an old debt. When the girls made their bid, I figured I'd buy them an ice cream cone and we'd call it a day.''

"No!"

Beth looked at Caleb, who'd been quiet during the whole discussion. She'd barely noticed him, skulking near the rack of dishes. But his objection got her attention. "What's wrong?"

Caleb looked at his shoes for a moment, then lifted his gaze to her. He was blushing, the pink on his cheeks like a deliberate brush stroke. "He's a master builder," he said, his voice so soft she barely heard him.

"Okay," she said gently, moving closer to her son. "Is there more, Caleb?"

He nodded, sending a quick, shy glance at Jarred, then lowering his head again. "He can help with the house."

Beth sighed, her heart squeezing tight as she finally got the picture. They'd bought him to help at the ranch. They'd bought him for her. Lord, how she wished she hadn't gotten them into this mess of a life. They deserved so much more. But she'd talk to Caleb and the twins later, when they were alone. Right now she had Mr. Universe to deal with. She turned.

"There's been a misunderstanding," she said, more relaxed now that she understood what was going on. "The children thought they were hiring you to do some work on our ranch."

"What kind of work?" he asked.

She shook her head. "I wouldn't even know where to begin. The whole place is old and broken. It doesn't matter. We'll take care of it ourselves. But thanks for being such a good sport."

"Jarred," a voice called from the door. "Just the man I was looking for."

Everyone turned, including the man in question. Beth watched Sam Duncan walk toward them with his familiar rolling gait. Such a welcome sight in his battered cowboy hat. She'd met the older man years ago, when she'd visited her grandfather's ranch. When she moved back to Lightning Creek, Wyoming, he was the first person she'd looked up. But right now, his gaze was fixed on Jarred, and as he grew near, Beth detected a curious twinkle in the old brown eyes.

"Sam," Jarred said, his voice almost a whisper.

Beth looked up at him, curious about his tone. It didn't seem as if a man like Jarred could whisper. Now that she saw his face, she knew Sam was important to him. Why, she didn't know, but somehow Sam managed to make the big man look smaller.

"How do, Beth," Sam said, tipping the brim of his hat. "Girls," he said to the twins. "Young fella," to Caleb. Then his gaze settled back on Jarred. "I'm happy to see you, son."

Jarred looked down, reminding Beth of Caleb. With the shock of loosened hair and the almost timid stance, Jarred seemed very young and vulnerable, which was an odd thing to think about such a large person.

"How are you, Sam?"

"I'm better after seeing you," the old man said. "I heard about the lovely ladies who bought you at the auction, and I came to see for myself."

Jarred stepped behind the girls, putting a large but gentle hand on each of their backs to scoot them forward. "This is Karen and Debbi," he said.

Sam looked down at them and smiled. "We're old friends, aren't we, ladies? You got yourself quite a catch there, didn't you?"

The girls, who had taken a shine to Sam ever since he'd let them ride one of his ponies, nodded in unison. "You know what?" Debbi said excitedly. He's—"

Karen reached over and pinched her sister's arm.

"Ow!" Debbi rubbed the sore spot and looked crossly at Karen. "What'd you do that for?"

"He's a master builder," Karen said, frowning at Debbi.

Debbi froze for a second. Then she smiled and nodded, as if she'd just decoded a secret message.

Jarred and Sam both looked confused, but Beth was used to their secrets. They didn't exactly have a language of their own, although they did tend to share the same sentences, one starting and the other finishing, and they had a great affinity for keeping to themselves, creating a world inhabited by two.

"He's gonna work on our house," Caleb said. "He has to. We bought him fair and square."

Beth touched her son on the arm, but he jerked away, his shoulders slouching in a protective and isolating move. She wished, for the hundredth time, that she could help him. He'd once been as open and friendly as the twins, but after his father had left them, he'd turned into a frightened little turtle. "We can't ask him to help on the house, sweetheart."

"Why not?" Caleb asked.

"Why not, indeed?" Sam said.

Beth looked at her old friend, but he didn't seem to be kidding.

"I think these children made a very wise purchase.

No man here could do a better job on those chores you've got waitin'."

"Hold on there, Sam," Jarred said. "Just hold on right there." He walked over to the long kitchen counter and pulled a folded-up wallet out of his back pocket. He opened it, found a check, then turned back to Beth. "Do you have a pen?"

She nodded, leaving the small group to get her purse from the lockers against the far wall. She watched her children and the two men as she fished in her bag until she found her pen. Sam smiled, and the girls smiled back. Caleb looked solemn and sad, and Jarred, he just looked anxious.

What was his story? Lost Springs Ranch for Boys provided a home for troubled youths, and he'd obviously lived here at some point in his life. Otherwise he wouldn't have been in the auction. He was a master builder, whatever that meant. And he had something to prove to Sam.

It was an interesting mystery. It occurred to her that it had been a long time since she'd had cause to wonder about grown men. It was almost…exciting.

She hurried back and handed Jarred the pen. He turned to his check and filled it out. After he'd signed his name, he handed her pen back and gave the check to Sam. "There," he said. "We're square. That takes care of everything."

Sam eyed the check for a moment, then looked up into Jarred's eyes. "No, son. I don't think so. I think you need to do this family a good turn, don't you?"

Jarred didn't say anything. He just glanced at Beth, at her children, his gaze lingering a bit on Caleb, then he faced Sam once more. "A good turn, huh?"

Sam nodded.

Jarred shook his head as if bemoaning his fate, then he sighed. "All right. But then we're square, right?"

"That'll be up to you," Sam said.

"Uh, excuse me?" Beth queried.

The men looked at her as if they'd forgotten she was there.

"This family doesn't need a stranger to do them a good turn, but thank you, anyway. Now, I have to get back to work. And my children have to go out and get something to eat."

Karen and Debbi whirled to face her, their expressions urgent and pleading. "You don't understand," Debbi said.

"We bought him for charity," Karen said. "Didn't you tell us charity was good?"

"Yes, I did. But I didn't mean that *we* needed the charity."

"But, Mom!" the girls protested, their voices a perfect match.

"Pardon me, ma'am," Jarred said, "but you've got it backward. You'd be doing *me* the favor."

"I don't get any of this," Beth said, intending to give him a quick and firm no. But then she looked at his eyes, and what she saw there changed her mind. If anything, he looked more desperate than the twins. There was a play going on, and she had no idea who was directing and who was in the audience. But if her instincts held true, Jarred was telling her the truth. She would be doing him a favor. She looked at Sam, at Caleb, at her twins, all of them waiting for her to say yes. "I guess I'm outnumbered," she said at last.

"Yeah!" The girls jumped up and down, as if she'd just promised they could go to Disneyland.

Caleb stood up a bit straighter, but he didn't give any other sign of his victory.

Jarred just looked resigned. Sam didn't gloat at all.

"How about you come out to the house next Saturday," Beth said.

Jarred shook his head. "I've got to get back to Houston as soon as possible. If it's okay with you, I'd like to work tomorrow."

Beth didn't have to think about it very long. The only thing she had planned for Sunday was working on the house, so Jarred might as well pitch in. "Okay," she said. "Tomorrow it is."

"Where do you live?"

"I'm at the old Whittaker place."

"Oh, yeah," he said, with a trace of wistfulness. "I was there once, a long time ago. Mr. Whittaker used to board horses."

"That's right. He was my grandfather."

"Really?"

She nodded. "He left me the ranch after he died."

"You looking to board horses, too?"

"No, I'm afraid I don't even remember how to ride. I'm converting the place into a bed-and-breakfast. That is, if I live through the remodeling."

For the first time since she'd seen him, Jarred looked interested instead of shanghaied. "What construction company are you working with?"

Smiling, she put her hands on the twins' shoulders. "Cochran and family."

"I don't know them," Jarred said.

"Yes, you do."

He thought for a moment, his dark brows coming slightly together while his pale blue eyes looked her over. Then his whole expression changed with understanding. "You guys, right?"

"Us guys," she agreed.

"You see," Sam said. "I told you he was just the man for the job. He's a hard worker. Always has been."

There it was again, the interplay between Sam and Jarred so rife with meaning she could almost see the years of history in their eyes.

Jarred cleared his throat, then stepped back. He gave a smile, though she didn't believe it was sincere, then nodded at her. "I'll see you first thing in the morning," he said.

"Great."

"Us, too?" Karen asked.

"Especially you," Jarred answered, his smile finally true. "I haven't forgotten who bought me."

Debbi and Karen looked at each other briefly, then Debbi crooked her finger, asking Jarred to come down. He got the idea and crouched down beside the girls. Debbi leaned forward and cupped her hands against his ear. She whispered something, and Jarred's eyes widened, making Beth mighty suspicious that her precocious six-year-old had just said something that would come back and bite Beth on the rear end.

Jarred rose, nodded one more time at the girls, then held out his hand to Sam. "It's good to see you again."

"I thank you for coming back," Sam said. "It's good to see how you've grown."

Jarred gave Sam a tight-lipped smile, then headed out of the kitchen. Beth watched him walk away, her gaze exploring the back of him, from the wide shoul-

ders to the trim waist and the long jeans-clad legs. A
very un-maternal thought popped into her mind, and
she felt the heat rise to her cheeks.

"I'd best be heading back to the barbecue," Sam
said.

Beth jerked her attention back to him, and she held
out her hand. He grabbed it, shaking it firmly, letting
her feel the lifetime of work etched on his palm.
"Thank you, Sam."

"No need. This is more for him than you, although
I'm glad you'll benefit."

"What's going on between you two?"

He smiled. "Maybe he'll tell you about it." Then
Sam looked at Caleb. "Good to see you, son."

Caleb nodded so slightly Beth might have imagined
it.

"And you little beauties," Sam said. "I'm counting on you to chaperone your mom."

"What's that mean?" Debbi asked.

"It means to keep your eyes and ears open."

Debbi and Karen nodded as if that job had always
been theirs. Which, Beth guessed, wasn't too far off
the mark.

"I'll be talkin' to you soon," Sam said, and then
he, too, headed toward the door.

Beth looked over at her sink. No one had added
any pots or dishes the whole time she'd had company.
Then she looked at Carol, the other woman hired for
the day. Her sink had a pile of plates so high they'd
topple with the June breeze. "I've got to get back to
work," she announced, turning to the kids. She
reached into her pocket and pulled out some money,
which she handed to her son. "Caleb, can I trust you
to make sure they eat like ladies?"

Caleb nodded.

"Okay, then. You guys go eat, and when you're finished, come back in here. I've got another hour or so of work before I can leave."

Debbi grabbed Karen's hand, and they made a beeline for the door. Caleb hung back a bit. She waited, knowing he wanted to tell her something privately. Finally, he turned his sorrowful brown eyes toward her. "You shouldn't be washing dishes," he whispered.

"Why not? It's an honest job for honest pay."

"Dad wouldn't let you do that."

Beth's chest constricted. Caleb had built his father into something far nobler than he was. And she didn't want to spoil his illusions unless she had to. "He probably wouldn't like it," she said, "but he'd understand that times are tough, and money scarce."

She could see Caleb wanted to say something more. That he wanted to scold her for moving to this wild country, into that horrible rickety house with the cracked walls and the holes in the ceiling. Instead, he closed his mouth up tight and walked away.

Beth fought the urge to go after him. She couldn't fix the hurt he was feeling even though she wanted to with her whole heart. He was on a lonely road, and she prayed he made it safely to the end.

The sound of loudly spraying water brought her back to the room, and to her job. She went over to Carol's sink and hefted a big stack of dishes. "Thanks," she said.

Carol nodded once and gave her a kindly smile.

Beth went back to her station and plunged into washing dishes. Her thoughts flew about for a moment, then landed squarely on a tall man with light-blue eyes and steady hands. She pictured his smile, how it changed his face. And then she thought about his shoulders. So big and wide, built for leaning on.

When was the last time she'd leaned on someone's shoulder? How nice would it feel to have those strong arms around her?

Hold on. She'd better stop that thought right there. The twins hadn't bought Jarred McCoy, they'd only rented him.

CHAPTER THREE

JARRED SAT ON HIS motel room bed, staring at his boxer shorts. He'd only brought two pairs, since he hadn't planned on staying. He'd stop by the General Store on his way to the ranch and pick up another, and maybe a T-shirt, too. The immediate problem solved, he looked up at the window and watched the sun work its way higher in the sky. His mind shifted to his bigger problem.

All he'd wanted to do was square things with Sam. It should have been easy. A check. An apology. A quick getaway.

Instead, he'd been roped into going out to *her* place. He was no expert on women, but he'd sized her up after ten minutes. She was the kind of woman who wore her heart on her sleeve. Nothing hidden. Nothing disguised. It was there in her eyes. The way she loved her kids, how she worried about the boy. Her determination to keep on going, even though she didn't have a husband.

The kids had said he was in San Diego. Probably ran off with his secretary or some such thing. Fool to leave a family like that behind, but then, Jarred didn't know the particulars.

He stood up and stretched, feeling the strain in his muscles. He hadn't worked out for a couple of weeks, and it was starting to tell. Moving to the space between the bed and the television, he continued stretching, but this time with a purpose. Back home, he usually went to the gym at least four times a week, hating it all the way. But he didn't have a choice. Now that the company had grown so large, he didn't do much physical labor. All he seemed to do these days was talk on the damn phone.

He got down on the floor, grabbed his feet and concentrated on relaxing his back. Thoughts of Beth tried to distract him, but he wouldn't listen. He just went through the routine that had been part of his life for years—stretching, relaxing, breathing.

It wasn't until he started his push-ups that she crashed through his mental barriers. It was easy to picture her, standing in that ugly apron, her blond hair all disheveled. Even like that, her looks appealed to him. Too much. It reminded him that it had been a long time since he'd been with a woman, especially a woman who piqued his interest as well as his libido.

He fought to focus again, but realized he'd lost count. His muscles burned, so he must have done at least fifty push-ups. He liked to do a hundred, but fifty was plenty for today.

Glancing at the motel's clock radio, he figured he'd have time for a shower, then some breakfast at the Main Street Grill. He hauled himself up, but he didn't head for the bathroom. Not yet. Instead, he went to the nightstand and opened the top drawer. The phone book was there, a slim volume, but then there weren't all that many residents in Lightning Creek. He flipped through the yellow pages quickly until he found it. The Main Street Grill—often referred to as the Roadkill Grill, although Jarred had always liked the food. It *was* still there. He wondered if they still served those thick chocolate malts he'd liked so much as a kid.

The memories made him sit down, they came rushing in so fast. He'd been a wild one, so full of piss and vinegar no one had known what to do with him. Sam had tried. Tried hard. The old man had taken him to the grill three or four times, bribing him with the malts, trying to get him to open up. But Jarred had kept his misery to himself. Maybe if he'd tried…

Jarred closed the phone book and stuck it back in the drawer. He'd thought writing that check would be enough. That once his debt was paid, he'd shake this town, these memories, for good. It hadn't happened. He still had more to do. He had to do a good turn for Beth Cochran and her family. Once that was finished, he'd be free. He had to be free. He had no intention of carrying that load of guilt through another sixteen years.

THOSE SAME SIXTEEN YEARS hadn't been kind to the Whittaker ranch. The place had been old when Jarred was a boy, and the brutal Wyoming winters had made their mark on the house. The barn was gone completely, along with the corral. But then Beth had said she didn't want to board horses.

He heard the taxi disappear down the dirt road as he made a first-glance inventory of the big house. The roof needed repair, if not complete replacement; there were at least two windows that had been covered by sheets of plywood. The porch sagged, and quite a few bricks had crumbled from the chimney.

On the bright side, the place had been carefully built back in the early 1900s. Good solid pine logs, as tough as the land they grew on, had weathered all storms. Whatever else needed fixing, the structure would stay sound.

His day's work would be a drop in the bucket. If Beth thought she and her kids could really renovate this place by themselves, she was in for a brutal awakening. If he'd been in charge of this operation, he'd plan on a ten-man crew working a couple of months.

But that wasn't his problem. All he had to do was lend a hand today, and then he could leave Lightning Creek for good. He hadn't liked it when he'd lived here before, and he didn't like it now.

He headed toward the house, letting his gaze wander to the view behind it. The Laramie Mountains flanked the left, and the Bighorn Mountains the right. The valley looked dry, but beautiful nonetheless. He'd give Lightning Creek points for scenery, but scenery didn't mean a whole lot to a lonely kid. It was just miles of mountains in the way.

The front door swung open with a loud creak, then a thud of wood on wood as the screen door whacked the side of the house. Karen and Debbi came tearing out of the house as if they were being chased by a bear. But the smiles on their faces told him they weren't running from, but to. He just had time to lift his overnight bag to his chest before the two little girls jumped on his legs, one each, wrapping themselves around him like shin guards. Their arms and legs were so tight, both girls were completely off the ground. It stopped him, and not just the weight of carrying two extra people. Something inside him was touched. He'd never had any kid act so happy to see him.

"We waited all morning!" Debbi said, looking straight up so she wouldn't have to let go of his leg.

"You took so long!" Karen cried, holding on so tightly she was starting to cut off his circulation.

"Nice to see you, too," he said, waiting for them to get down.

Neither of them seemed the least bit ready to do that, however. They just hung on for dear life and shrieked with laughter.

There was nothing to do but go on. He lifted his right leg, and Debbi with it, and took one lumbering step. She squealed as if he was the best ride since Space Mountain.

He repeated the process with his left leg, and Karen matched her twin's shriek right down to the pitch.

Step by step, he headed toward the house. The noise reached earsplitting decibels, the laughter threatening to loosen the girls' grips. Jarred joined in, unable to keep a straight face as he made his ponderous way.

"What in the world?"

He looked up. There, in the doorway, stood Beth. He met her gaze, heard her laugh. Her smile made him feel completely self-conscious and amazingly accepted, both at the same time.

"Girls!" Beth shouted. "How many times have I told you *not* to ride on the company!"

He walked faster, raising and lowering each leg in great arcs, thrilling his jockeys and obviously delighting their mother. Too soon, he reached the porch, and first Debbi, then Karen let go, sliding down the brief distance to hit the hard earth with two little *thunks*.

Beth hadn't taken her eyes off him. Her laughter dimmed, but her smile didn't. It made her look like she was eighteen. A very pretty eighteen.

"That was one heck of an entrance," she said.

"The next show is at noon." He stepped onto the porch, aware of the creak of wood underneath him but spellbound by what lay ahead.

"What do you do for an encore?" she asked, her voice smaller and a lot more intimate.

"I don't want to spoil the surprise," he said.

She opened her mouth, just a little. Just enough for him to see the tips of her even white teeth. He wasn't near enough to hear her sharp breath, but he saw the rise of her chest, then no movement at all while his heart beat six times. Finally, she exhaled, exchanging her held breath for a flush of pink on her cheeks.

He liked that a lot.

"Mom," Karen said, interrupting the...whatever it was. Beth blinked, then looked down at Karen, who'd climbed on the porch and grabbed hold of the side of Beth's jeans.

"What?"

"You know."

Beth stared at her daughter for a long moment. Then she looked at him, as if she'd just remembered something. "The girls made you a present," she said.

"Really?"

Not to be outdone by Karen, Debbi got up and went to her mother's other side. Like bookends. Their clothes weren't identical. Karen wore overalls and Debbi had on pink shorts and a T-shirt, but that didn't detract from the amazing likeness. He was surprised he didn't have more trouble telling them apart. Their blond hair was long and held back by head bands, blue for Karen, pink for Debbi. They had tiny little noses and great big green eyes, and each of them had a dimple, Karen's on the right, Debbi's on the left. Mirror images themselves, they were also amazingly like their mother. Pretty enough to cause havoc with the male population, even at age six.

"Come *on*," Debbi said, her impatience urging them all into action. Beth walked into the house, still flanked by the girls, and he followed. The scent of cinnamon hit him immediately, filling him with a nostalgia for a past he'd only dreamed of. A warm family kitchen, siblings of his own...

The living room was sparsely furnished. An old television set with a rabbit-ear antenna, a floral-patterned couch and three beanbag chairs. There was only one lamp, but seven boxes of books. He spotted a Barbie and a Game Boy on the floor next to the crumbling fireplace. There were more boxes against the far wall and tools in a heap on a big tarp.

He felt a tug on his leg, and saw that Beth and Debbi had moved on toward the kitchen. Small fingers curled around his thumb, then gave him a sharp tug. He followed obediently, letting go of his desire to look at the house. There would be time for that later. After his surprise.

Once inside the spacious kitchen, he saw a plate piled high with something, covered by an opened napkin. The twins stood on either side of the prize, each taking a small corner of the napkin between thumb and forefinger. On some silent cue, they lifted the cover to reveal a stack of muffins. Oddly shaped muffins, with blueberries and nuts dotting the dark cake.

"We made them by ourself," Debbi said.

"Mom turned on the oven," Karen added.

"But we used the mixer, and we did everything right the first time."

Jarred smiled, just now noticing the mess on the tile counters. Empty eggshells, flour, measuring cups and a mixing bowl made him aware of what a big project this had been for the girls. "I'm impressed," he said. "They look wonderful."

"Eat one!" Karen said, almost shaking in her excitement.

Jarred reached over and plucked the top muffin. He examined the lopsided treat, nodding as if he were looking at a precious gem. Then he took a bite. His acting changed to real enthusiasm as he chewed. The muffins might look funny but they tasted great. He swallowed, then turned to the girls. "I'm pretty sure these are the best muffins I've ever had. No, wait. I'm positive. They're the best."

The girls exchanged a look of pure bliss, then ran over and locked their arms around his legs, nearly knocking him over in their enthusiasm.

His gaze turned to Beth, who stood leaning against the far counter, arms crossed over her T-shirt, the smile on her face as loving a thing as he'd ever seen.

"Girls," she said. "It's time."

They both moaned in unison and clutched him tighter.

"Come on. Let go of Mr. McCoy. We have work to do."

"Aw, Mom," Karen whined.

"Can't we just have one more muffin?" Debbi pleaded.

"You've had more than enough," Beth said. She approached Jarred, but her gaze stayed fixed on the girls. "Outside. Now."

"But, Mom!" Debbi let him go and turned all her attention to swaying her mother.

"Don't 'but Mom' me. You know the arrangement.

I want the two of you outside, and I want you to have a good time. That's an order.''

Karen let go in an exaggerated surrender. She frowned deeply and started toward the back door, slumped forward, tennis shoes shuffling. Debbi mimicked her down to the frown, but finally they made it to the door, and with one plaintive look back, they went to carry out their sentence.

"You were pretty rough on them," Jarred said.

"I know. I'm a horrible mother. What can I say?"

He looked at her, wanting to tell her that he thought she must be the best mother he'd ever seen. That even though he'd only known her a day, he could feel the love she had for her children, the extraordinary care she gave them. But he couldn't say those things. Not out loud. Not to a stranger.

"How about some coffee?" she asked.

He nodded, grateful that she'd turned to the pot on the counter.

"You've really made an impression on the girls," she told him as she reached into the cupboard for two mugs.

"I can see that," he said. "What I don't understand is why."

"I'm not positive, but I think it has something to do with the fact that you're a builder. It's been pretty tough on them, all this remodeling business. I think they think you're going to rescue us all."

He put his muffin down on the table. "I wish that were true. But I'm afraid I won't be able to do all that in one day."

She shrugged. "Of course not. It's wonderful of you to do this at all. You really didn't have to."

"Of course I did. They paid for me fair and square."

She turned to look at him, her eyes narrowed and her brow furrowed. "Why do I get the feeling this had nothing to do with the auction and everything to do with Sam?"

"Because it's true. I owed him a favor."

"Oh?"

He knew she wanted him to explain. But that was another wish he wasn't going to fulfill. He wasn't proud of his debt to Sam, and he certainly wasn't going to admit his faults to Beth. Not when things were going so nicely.

"Cream?"

"Hmm?"

"Your coffee."

"Oh, no, thanks. Black is fine."

She handed him a mug from the San Diego library. Then she lifted her own, this one with a picture of a cat, and took a sip. Her lips barely touched the rim of the cup, pursing slightly, then relaxing. They looked incredibly soft, those lips. Soft and tender and sweet...

"So at least tell me why you put yourself up for auction," she said.

He jerked his gaze from her lips, then took a drink of his own coffee. Too big a drink. Too hot a drink. He turned away, trying to act casual as he grimaced in pain. By the time he looked at her again, his face was under control. But the slight grin on the lips that had gotten him into trouble in the first place told him Beth had seen through his little act. "I grew up there," he said, not willing to admit complete defeat.

"Oh?"

He nodded. "I was orphaned at nine. I lived there until I was sixteen."

"I see."

He thought about telling her more. About what a wild kid he'd been. How he'd given Sam more hell than any three boys put together. But why tell her when he was leaving so soon? What good would it do?

"How about a tour of the house?" she asked, letting the more personal question go unasked.

"Sure."

She looked around the big kitchen, shaking her head at the mess on the counter. "Normally, it's neater in here. But you can see that the wall behind the stove needs replacing, and the floor is warped. I won't even discuss the plumbing."

"How's your electricity?"

"Spotty at best. We can't run the can opener and the vacuum at the same time."

He nodded. "It's not surprising. These old houses weren't built by contractors. I'd be surprised if your grandfather didn't wire the house himself."

"I think it was his father, actually," Beth said. "This place is almost a hundred years old."

"The frame is solid, though. And that's a good start."

She sighed. "I just wish I knew more. I've gotten the whole Time-Life series on remodeling. That helps."

"It's a big job."

She nodded. "I'm a big girl. It may take me a year, but I'll get it done. You just watch."

He smiled at her earnestness. It reminded him so

much of the twins. "I don't doubt it for a moment. But let's you and me go see what I can do to help."

"Follow me," she said.

He grabbed his half-eaten muffin from the table and let his gaze travel down her back as she led him into the hallway. Her jeans enhanced the heart shape of her bottom, small, like her, and perfect. Such a tiny thing to have such a big load on her shoulders. But he'd spoken the truth. He didn't doubt she could do whatever she had to. Including remodeling this old rickety house. He just wished he lived closer so he could do it for her.

As she turned the corner into a bedroom, he realized what he'd been thinking. Do it for her? He barely knew the lady. He hated the town she lived in. Hell, most of the time, he didn't even like kids.

Crazy, that's all. Just plain crazy.

CHAPTER FOUR

BETH LOOKED AROUND Caleb's bedroom, saddened to see it so neat. Not that she didn't like things tidy, but for Caleb, it wasn't good. Although he hadn't said anything, she knew he wanted to be ready to leave at a moment's notice. So he lived as though he were in a hotel, keeping his clothes folded in a box instead of using the perfectly good dresser she'd brought from San Diego. He had a neat stack of comic books by the side of his bed, a baseball and glove on the little desk. Everything else was in the closet. Even the Chewbacca and Han Solo posters he'd loved so much sat curled into tight tubes, resting against his winter coat.

"The guest room?"

She shook her head, moving her gaze up to meet Jarred's. "Caleb's room."

"Really?"

His surprise was another arrow in her heart. "He's…he hasn't really settled in yet."

"How old is he, nine?"

She nodded.

"That can be a tough age. Especially if there's been a big change."

"Like a divorce."

Jarred nodded, his light-blue eyes, so startling

against his dark coloring, sympathetic and kind. "How long has it been?"

"We've been here four months."

"No wonder he's having a hard time. Four months isn't very long, especially for a kid. If I remember correctly, a year went on forever at nine."

Beth went over to the bed and sat on the *Star Wars* quilt. She hated that the floor was uncarpeted and that it buckled like a roller coaster. She hated the patched walls and the sheet of plywood over the window. "He misses his dad," she said. "He doesn't understand."

"A divorce isn't easy for an adult to understand."

"Actually, we're not divorced. Not officially. The papers have all been drawn up but..."

"You don't want to give up?"

She shook her head, more vehemently than she meant to. "No, no, I do give up. It's the best thing, trust me. Only Caleb thinks things are...different."

Jarred squatted down to examine the floorboards. Even when he was crouched so low, he still looked tall. His head would come all the way up to her chest if she stood next to him. He ran long fingers over the warped wood, his touch light and so delicate it made her back tingle.

"This will end up being my room. I'm planning on painting it a light, light mauve with white lace curtains to go with my grandmother's bedspread." She pointed to the desk. "I want to replace that with a real workstation. A place I can pay the bills and keep the files. And I want the window to be bigger, if it's possible. I want to be able to look out and see the trees."

He nodded, then turned his attention back to the floor. "This is all going to have to go," he said. His gaze lifted as he surveyed the rest of the room. "The walls need work. The ceiling's bad. I'd replace that closet door, too."

She scrutinized him the same way he looked at the room. Such a handsome man. Too handsome. She'd never been interested in gorgeous guys because every one she knew had sailed through life. They'd been treated like kings, and not just by adoring girls. Teachers, parents, everyone always gave the handsome ones the benefit of the doubt. They thought they could get away with murder, and it was almost always true.

But Jarred didn't seem to have that air of cockiness she usually saw in a hunk. Maybe it was because he'd been orphaned. Maybe that had been the fire that tempered his steel. Besides, Sam cared about him. She knew Sam well enough to recognize the signs. And if he cared, then Jarred was someone worth caring about.

"Is this where you want to start?"

She shook her head. "No, I guess not. I think we should concentrate on the dining room wall. I want to knock it down and extend it into the back bedroom."

"Do you have blueprints?"

"Sure. You want to see?"

"If you don't mind."

She stood up, and he did, too, surprising her again with his height and his breadth. It was a wonder he fit through the doorway.

"They're in my room," she said, leading him to the staircase. She climbed, terribly aware of him behind her, of what he was looking at. She should have worn a skirt, not these old ratty jeans, but then that would have looked ridiculous. She was about to attack a wall with a sledgehammer. Heels and panty hose would have been a bit much.

She reached the second-floor landing and led Jarred down the hall toward the master suite. "Careful of the railing," she warned. "It's not steady."

"The wood's rotten," he said. "It'll have to be replaced."

"It's on the list," she said. "The very, very long list."

At her bedroom door, she paused until he caught up with her. He looked concerned, and she hoped it was just that he was thinking deeply, not that he was going to tell her something unpleasant about the house. She didn't have a plan B. She barely had a plan A.

"In here," she said, walking past her bed to the old desk by the side wall. The blueprints were right on top. She'd had to learn to read them. Books on remodeling, construction, woodworking, plumbing, electrical wiring and all the other skills she'd need lined two bookshelves by her bed.

"You really aren't kidding about this, are you?"

"Nope."

He shook his head, as if wondering about her sanity. She didn't blame him. She wondered about it herself.

"I want to turn this floor into guest rooms. As authentically Old West as I can without sacrificing amenities."

"What about the kids' rooms?"

"They'll be upstairs, in the attic. It's large, but it'll probably have to be extended. The girls want to share, so I need room enough for two canopy beds. Shelves for their dolls.'' She smiled. ''They insist on yellow. Nothing else will do. I suppose it can work, if I use a lot of white for accessories.''

''That's good,'' he said. ''Tell me what you know you want. Then I can see if it's possible.''

''For the whole house?''

He nodded.

She got comfy and began, starting from the attic and moving room to room. The plans she'd been mulling over for months became so clear she could almost see the finished product. A home for her family. A refuge for her guests. It all seemed possible, telling it like this.

Jarred listened intently, and as soon as she finished, his focus moved to the blueprint, and she was forgotten. His concentration was total. He leaned over the desk, bracing his hands on the wood. His brows came down and he frowned. She let herself study him, from the way his hair curled around his ear to the cord of muscle in his neck. Down to his shoulder, so broad and round it was as if he were wearing shoulder pads.

From her angle, she mostly got the side view, and it wasn't enough. Quietly, afraid to disturb him, she stepped back until she could see his rear. It wasn't fair that he had such a trim waist and slim hips. Although, she had to admit, it was something to behold. The inverted V from shoulder to waist was one of the most masculine images she'd seen. Kind of like a football player in uniform, only Jarred's pads were all muscle and sinew. She contemplated his butt for a moment. Round, firm, perfect for squeezing. Then there were his legs, with those strong thighs. Oh, heavens...

What would he look like naked? Her gaze snapped to his hands. Long, thick fingers. Damn.

She took in a great breath of air, then let it out slowly as she moved back to her original position. At the end of her breath, she looked at his face and found that his frown had been replaced by a broad grin. And he wasn't looking at the blueprints any longer. He stared straight ahead....

Into the mirror. The big full-length mirror that gave him an excellent view of the room behind him. He'd watched her watching him. Seen how she lusted after him. No way had he missed her licking her lips as she checked out his behind.

The heat started in her cheeks, then spread to her face and neck. She felt sure if she looked down, she'd see that her feet had turned red.

"So, uh, this is the wall you want removed?" Jarred asked, pointing at the blueprint.

She didn't even bother looking. She just nodded.

"Great. You've got enough support to take it down without any structural damage."

Although his words were all business, there was no mistaking the amusement in his voice. She thought about asking him to leave. But that would just make it worse. "What next?" she said, her voice higher than normal, but at least she didn't squeak.

"We find the sledgehammers," he said. He stood and turned fully toward her. He worked hard at not smiling—she could see the corner of his lips twitch. But he couldn't hide the delight in his eyes.

"I, uh…I." She stopped sputtering, resigned to her humiliation. If he'd only turn back around. Or disappear. She buried her head in her hands, unable to look at him for one more second.

His soft chuckle didn't help. Neither did the gentle hand on her shoulder. She just turned, her face still covered, so her back was to him.

"Beth," he whispered.

She took another step away.

"I checked you out, too," he said. "You just didn't see 'cause you were walking up the stairs."

She groaned in acute misery. Knowing he'd given her the once-over, and from the rear, no less, didn't ease her embarrassment. It just made things worse.

"I liked what I saw, Beth," he continued. "If I wasn't leaving tonight... You're quite the babe."

She whirled to face him, not dropping her hands, but separating her fingers so she could see him. "Really?" she said, her voice muffled by her palms.

"Really," he said.

She studied his smile. It seemed genuine. But then, what was he going to say? "Seeing you from behind made me rethink my sexual preference?"

He reached over and took her wrists in his hands. They circled her neatly, they were so big, but he was extremely gentle. As if he were handling something delicate. He moved her hands down, away from her face, forcing her to look right into his light-blue eyes.

"I'm flattered," he said. "At least, I think I am. You did like what you saw, didn't you?"

She nodded. "Gosh, yes."

He chuckled again, a deep, masculine sound. "Then we're even."

She nodded, too, trying to will the fire from her cheeks.

"What say we work off some of this energy by knocking down a wall."

"Yes," she said, so anxious to get on with it, she

darted toward the door. But he still had her wrists, stopping her just as her right shoulder touched his left arm.

"Beth?"

"Yes?" She stared straight ahead as her heart thudded in her chest.

"I… Never mind," he said, releasing her. "Nothing."

She chanced one more glance at him. His gaze was on her face, and his amusement had vanished. Something else was in his eyes. Hunger. Need.

She walked away as quickly as she could without actually running. Instead of going downstairs to start work, she dashed into the bathroom and locked the door behind her. Suddenly weak, she went to the bathtub and sat on the rim.

What in the world had come over her?

She hadn't reacted to a man like this since… She'd *never* reacted to a man like this. Not even Dan, when she'd first met him. Although it bothered her a lot that Jarred had caught her ogling, it bothered her a lot more that she had, indeed, ogled! She'd looked him over like a prize bull, and lusted after him like…like… She didn't even know. But not like her. Not like any part of her she'd known before.

She'd actually been *aroused.* If she'd been a guy, she would have popped the buttons on her jeans. As it was, she felt herself tighten, the need to squeeze her legs together overpowering.

Holy cow, what was going on?

She stood up and went to the sink, turning on the cold water, watching it change from rust-brown to clear. She bent over and splashed her face, trying to cool herself down, or at least get rid of her blush.

After a few minutes, she stopped splashing and stood up and groped for a towel. When she felt reasonably dry, she looked at her image in the mirror. Okay, she had a grip. For the moment. Now, all she had to do was go downstairs and knock a wall down. Which would have been fine if she didn't have to do it right next to *him*.

She opened the door and heard banging downstairs. He'd obviously found the sledgehammer. Good. She'd have to put on a dust mask and so would he. They'd both concentrate on the work, and not on each other. Good again.

She could do this.

After all, he was leaving tonight, and she'd never see him again. Her humiliation would be private and, in time, would fade away to nothing.

JARRED TOOK ANOTHER mighty swing at the wall. Just as the hammer connected, he saw something dart past the hallway. He wasn't positive, he'd only caught it out of the corner of his eye, but he thought it was one of the twins.

He lifted the hammer again, positioning himself to achieve the maximum amount of energy, and let her rip.

There it was again. A flash of pink. The girls were inside, playing hide-and-go-seek. That had to stop. They could get hurt.

He'd mention it to Beth when she came down. If she ever came down. He smiled as he thought of her pink cheeks. He'd never seen anyone get quite so red. On another woman, it might have been unattractive, but on Beth? She looked damn fine.

No doubt about it, she was an attractive woman.

He couldn't help but think about what she'd be like in his bed. So tiny—he'd have to be careful not to hurt her.

His palm would cover her breast easily. He could span her waist with his hands. She could ride him like a pony, and he'd only feel one thing.

Jarred looked around, remembering that the girls were in the house. Not that they would know what he was thinking, but he didn't like the idea of having such lascivious thoughts around Beth's kids.

He swung the hammer again, feeling the reverberation all the way up his arms and down his back. It felt good, satisfying. He needed to use up some of his energy, and this was a very safe way to do just that.

Again and again, he swung the hammer, finding his rhythm, watching the plaster explode and scatter. With every strike, his thoughts grew bolder, the image of Beth beneath him grew stronger. He didn't want to stop. Ever.

But he did when he caught sight of something white in his peripheral vision. Midway through a swing, he froze. But it wasn't one of the twins. It was Beth.

The fringe of hair around her face was damp, as if she'd just washed. She barely looked at him. Instead, she grabbed one of the dust masks from the floor and put it on, hiding her nose and mouth. It was an ugly thing, white and utilitarian. But she still managed to look really good.

She glanced at him quickly, then lifted the smaller sledgehammer. Standing right next to him, she lifted it high in the air, then swung with all her might. It did some damage, but not enough. Her stance was all wrong.

He tapped her shoulder, and she swung around so fast he thought she was going to cripple him with the hammer. He stopped it with his hand before it made contact. "You're doing it wrong," he said, his voice muffled by his own mask.

"How can I be doing it wrong? It's a sledgehammer."

"Your stance," he said. "Let me show you."

Her brow furrowed as he walked around her, but she didn't move to stop him. He put his hammer down, took off his mask, then moved in close. So close, he touched her from his chest to his thighs. So close that he could smell the lilac in her hair.

"You're holding it too low," he said, his voice softening to a whisper. He put his arms around her shoulders and guided her hands to the correct position. My God, she was like a little bird.

His gaze moved from her fingers to her neck. The plain T-shirt she wore was nothing but white cotton, but from his point of view, looking straight down her chest, the material molded perfectly over her breasts. They didn't need satin or silk to make them enticing. She could have been wearing a potato sack and he would have wanted her as much.

"Is there a next part to this process, or are we going to just stand here and admire my accomplishment?"

Jarred coughed, although he felt sure she knew exactly what had preoccupied him. It wasn't so terrible. She'd done it to him, right?

"Jarred?"

"Sorry." He scooted back a bit, so he wasn't touching her lower half. She didn't need to know his current predicament. "Spread your legs."

"What?"

He closed his eyes and took a deep breath. "Your feet are too close together. You need to widen them to get the full power of your back muscles into the swing."

"Oh." Beth widened her stance while he focused on the wall, on the hammer, on anything but the woman in front of him.

"Now, when you swing, pretend you're hitting a specific target. Don't just let it go willy-nilly."

"No willy-nilly," she said, gently mocking him. "Got it."

"That's good. You don't want to waste your energy, so take a deep breath as you pull the hammer back, and let it go as you swing. Lean forward, putting all your weight behind it."

"Breathe and lean. Check."

He stepped away, grateful for the distance. Anxious to get back to smashing the wall so he could release some of the tension in his body.

"Go for it," he said.

He watched her take her breath, but she blew out the air first, then swung. She leaned so far that she almost lost her footing. The hammer connected, but only by accident.

"Damn," she said, getting back into position.

"Don't worry about it. You'll get the hang of it. It's just a matter of rhythm, that's all.

She swung again, and this time, she did everything right. Her stance, her breath, the way she held the hammer. A huge hole sprang in the wall in front of her, and she yelped happily. "I did it!"

He grinned. "You sure did."

"I wanna do it again."

"It's all yours."

She took another big whack at the wall, her aim utterly true. For such a little thing, she packed quite a wallop.

"This is great," she said, swinging away like Casey at the bat.

"It is great, and you're doing a heck of a job, but there's no way we're finishing this up today."

She stopped and turned toward him. "Really?"

He shook his head. "Sorry."

"Oh, well," she said. "We'll get a good start."

He looked at her, dust coating her like powdered sugar. Her eyes bright and round and beautiful.

"I'd better go call the motel," he said.

"Pardon?"

"The motel. I'm gonna stick around another day or so. I don't have to rush back. And I did promise Sam." He looked around for a phone, but she must not have had one in the living room.

"You don't have to do this," Beth said. She pushed back her dust mask so it sat on top of her blond head, looking pretty silly.

"I know I don't have to. I want to."

"Oh."

"So, if you'll tell me where the phone is, I'll go call the motel and see if they'll let me stay another night."

"No!"

Jarred whirled around at the sharp cry. The twins popped up from behind some boxes of books, sharing a look of great consternation.

"You can't!" Debbi said.

"You can't!" Karen echoed an octave higher.

"You don't want him to stay?" Beth asked.

The little girls shook their heads as if they'd rehearsed the move for weeks. "He has to stay *here*," Karen said.

Beth stared at her daughters, then at him, then back at the girls. "Here?"

"Here," Debbi repeated. "In the attic."

"I don't think Mr. McCoy wants to sleep in an attic, girls."

"I don't mind," he said.

"He doesn't mind!" the twins cried together.

Beth took one more look at all the players. "All right, if you say so."

Debbi and Karen jumped up and down, hugging each other and giggling like mad. Beth looked worried, which he completely understood. And then he caught sight of the last member of their little gang. Caleb. Standing in the hallway, quiet as a mouse. Looking as if he wanted to blow the whole house to smithereens, and Jarred with it.

All Jarred wanted to do tonight was spend more time with Beth. But he finally understood why Sam had wanted him to come out here. Looking at Caleb was like looking at himself all those years ago. He understood the boy's pain and anger. He understood the feeling of helplessness. Caleb needed someone to talk to, and there was no way Jarred was going back to Texas before he gave it his best shot. But, hey, maybe he could spend some time with Beth, too. Like, after the kids were in bed.

CHAPTER FIVE

BETH FOLLOWED JARRED'S concerned gaze and saw Caleb in the hallway. He wore his anger like a cape, as if all the troubles in the world rested on his shoulders. "Excuse me," she said, taking the dust mask off her head and putting it down next to her sledgehammer. She walked toward Caleb, watching him make his decision to run or stay his ground. He stayed.

"Hi," she said.

He grunted in return, his frown deepening as he stared at a spot on the floor.

"Something wrong?"

He shrugged. God, how she hated that little movement. It gave her nothing, and it made her want to shake him. But he needed patience now, and heaven help her, she would give that to him. Even though she felt more helpless than any mother should. "Is it Jarred?"

Caleb looked up at her, just for a moment, but in that flash she saw his fury.

"I thought you wanted him to come here? To help us."

"He doesn't have to *stay* here."

Ah. The clue she'd been looking for. Now it made sense—at least a Caleb sort of sense. "He's going to stay in the attic," she said, desperate to touch her boy but knowing he'd shake her off like a mosquito. "Perfectly proper. No one will raise an eyebrow, I promise."

"What if—" He cut himself off, not willing to show so much of his vulnerability. But she knew what he was asking.

"Daddy won't be dropping in tonight," she said. "Or tomorrow. He's in San Diego, sweetheart."

"How do you know?"

"Because I spoke to him," she said, begging forgiveness for the lie. She hadn't spoken to Dan in days. Weeks. She couldn't. He was on a cruise with his new girlfriend. Not giving his family a moment's thought. But she couldn't tell Caleb that. Not when he wanted his father so badly. Not when he lived and breathed his wish for his father to come home.

"When?" Caleb asked, suspicion finally making him look her in the eyes.

"Last night," she said. "When you were asleep. He's on a business trip, Caleb. All the way to Mexico."

Caleb tried hard not to show his disappointment, but he wasn't old enough yet to mask his pain. She saw it in his lips, pressed tightly together lest they tremble. In the flush of his cheeks, and mostly in the shadow that fell over his eyes.

Every molecule in her longed to hug him. But she knew he'd run if she so much as reached out her hand.

"So are we okay with Jarred staying tonight?"

The shrug again. Just the shrug.

"It's going to be okay, Caleb," she whispered, praying this wasn't another lie. "I promise."

He didn't look at her. He simply turned, his rubber-soled tennis shoes squeaking on the uneven floor, and headed for his prison cell of a bedroom.

Of all the things Dan had done to her, no tragedy was greater than the pain he'd caused Caleb. For that, she wanted Dan punished. Hurt just as deeply in return. She'd tried convincing herself to let go of her anger. It didn't hurt him, but it ate her up inside. But she couldn't help it. Not when she saw her little boy's eyes.

"Mom?"

She turned to see Debbi and Karen standing at the edge of the hallway. They looked up at her, two beautiful faces needing reassurance and comfort. Beth sighed, wishing she was better at this. Wishing she knew some answers—any answers. All she could do was stumble her way through and hope that her kids came out all right.

For now, though, she crouched down and held out her arms. The twins rushed her like linebackers, nearly knocking her on her behind. The hug she gave them was filled with all her love, and what she got back in return was a double dose for herself.

"Is he going to stay?" Debbi whispered.

"Is he?" Karen echoed.

Beth nodded, gave the girls another squeeze, then stood up. She crossed her arms and scowled fiercely at the twins. "What I want to know is what you two were doing in the house?"

Karen looked at Debbi. Debbi looked at Karen. Then, as one, they spun on their heels and ran through the mess of a living room, screeching their terror as they headed for the door. They left with a crash, their laughter lingering like the dust from the broken plaster.

"Everything okay?"

Beth nodded, still staring at the door. Then she pasted on a smile and faced her guest. He had his hammer in his hands and the mask on top of his head. The way he looked at her—so concerned, so anxious—made her laugh.

"What's wrong?"

She shook her head as she walked back to the living room. "You wouldn't understand."

"Try me."

She stood inches from him, which forced her to raise her chin high if she wanted to see his face. "You don't want to know."

His brows came down as he considered her words, then put the hammer back down. "I'm pretty sure I do."

"Why?"

"I don't know."

"Good answer," she said, teasing.

"Hey, at least it's honest."

She looked down again, settling on a view of his chest for the moment. "Fair enough," she said. "I laughed because you looked at me as if you cared."

"Why was that funny?"

"Not funny. Ironic. Tragic. It just never happened with…"

"Your ex?"

She nodded. Then she picked up her dust mask and put it on, ending the conversation. No need to spill her troubles onto Jarred's shoulders, even though they looked big enough to handle them. He was a guest. A visitor. A man who worked with his hands. And he'd be gone in a day.

Jarred followed her example and suited up once

more. He walked over to his area of the wall and lit into it with a crash. She got into position, and this time, instead of hitting just a wall, she pictured Dan's head. Using every ounce of muscle she had, she swung the hammer so hard, half the wall shattered.

THE WALL CAME TUMBLING DOWN. All of it. Of course, it now lay crumbled on the floor and the edges were a mess, but where there once were two small rooms, there was now just one large space. Jarred couldn't believe how much Beth had done. He'd figured she would work for an hour or two, then stop when the pain in her shoulders and back got too bad. But she hadn't. The only time she'd stopped was when she'd fixed tuna sandwiches for lunch.

He put his dust mask down and stretched, trying to ease the strain in his muscles. There had been a time when this kind of work wouldn't have made him break a sweat, but he'd grown soft from sitting in meetings and taking business lunches. His regular workouts at the gym couldn't prepare him for this. His back muscles felt on fire, and he knew it would be worse tomorrow.

If he felt this bad, what was it like for Beth?

He looked over at her. Her arms were up over her head in a stretch. She leaned back, wincing. She was covered with powdered plaster, her hair sticking up in a wild mess of blonde.

"You need a bath," he said.

She stopped her stretch to look at him. "You don't look so hot yourself, big guy."

He grinned. "That's not what I meant. You need a hot bath so you won't have to go to the hospital tomorrow. You worked too hard today."

"We got the wall down, didn't we?"

"We sure did. But I'm serious. You do need to be careful or you'll cripple yourself."

She dropped her arms, wincing again at the movement. "You're right. I'm happy to say that we now have hot water here, which we didn't for the first two weeks. So that's a plus."

"Yeah. Hot water can really come in handy."

"So what about you?" she asked. "I suppose this was a walk in the park, eh?"

"Oh, no. I need a bath, too." Then he almost said it. The words were on the tip of his tongue, but he caught himself just in time. She'd have kicked him out on his rear if he'd suggested they bathe together, but dammit, the idea was there, illustrated in living color by his overactive imagination.

"We have two," she said. "I'll use the one upstairs, and you can use the tub down here."

He looked around, not for anything in particular, just to hide the guilt written all over his face. The place looked as if it had been bombed, but his practiced gaze saw how much they'd done, and what the room would look like when it was finished. When he dared look at Beth again, he had to struggle not to laugh. She had pink cheeks again, that same blush she'd shown him upstairs. What do you know? She was thinking about that coed bath, too.

"Anyway," she said, turning so quickly she almost knocked over a stack of boxes. "There are towels in the bathroom."

"Thank you."

"We'll have dinner as soon as we're done," she said, her words coming fast and furious. "The girls can bathe later. Caleb can wait till tomorrow. But we'll all go to bed early tonight.''

She made it to the staircase and gave him one last embarrassed look before she rushed upstairs.

Jarred shook his head as he headed for the kitchen to get his overnight bag. He'd phoned the airport earlier to change his flight. This little act of penance was turning into something he hadn't counted on. Instead of feeling relieved that he was finally paying Sam his debt, all Jarred could think of was what he'd like to do with one very dusty woman. None of his thoughts were particularly penitent. In fact, he'd probably need to work here a week just to clear his conscience. But then, a week here with Beth wouldn't solve the problem. On the contrary, it would make things much, much worse.

He rounded the corner to the kitchen and saw that someone had moved his bag from the floor to the table. That was odd. Beth had probably done it while she'd made lunch. It must have been in her way. But why put it on the table?

The mystery would have to wait. He needed to get into a tub, and fast. With the hottest water he could stand. He grabbed his bag and it flew open, his clothes and toiletries flying all over the kitchen.

As he picked them up, his curiosity built. She'd opened his suitcase. Why? What had she been looking for? And why hadn't she closed it properly when she'd finished?

Very odd. Kind of spooky. But intriguing. After the kids went to bed, maybe Beth would tell him what she'd been up to.

BETH EASED INTO the hot water, grimacing as her muscles screamed at her. She sighed as she stretched out all the way and leaned her head against the plastic bath pillow. The heat made an immediate difference, and she willed herself to relax.

It occurred to her that Jarred wasn't going to be able to stretch out in the tub downstairs. It would be like bathing in a sink for him. His legs would stick out when he soaked his back, if he could even get down that low. Poor guy. He'd need a custom-made tub, wouldn't he?

She closed her eyes, picturing the man downstairs in a tub large enough for two. Naked and wet, beautiful and big. She'd wash his back slowly, using lots of lather, and then she'd drop the washcloth and use her hands to massage his wide shoulders. She'd knead his muscles like bread dough as he sat in front of her. Her legs circling his waist...

She opened her eyes, completely shocked at her X-rated thoughts. Something was seriously wrong here. Granted, he was a nice guy, and yes, he was very good-looking, but come on! Her mind hadn't been out of the gutter since he'd shown up this morning. It wasn't like her at all.

She'd only been with one man. And although sex had been pleasant in the beginning, it had never been something she'd yearned for. When she and Dan had stopped sleeping together after the twins were born, she'd been grateful, and she hadn't missed it at all.

Or so she thought.

But maybe she *had* missed sex. Maybe the troubles she had with Dan had smothered any flame of passion. If that were so, then it was clear Jarred had sparked her pilot light again. Pilot light, hell. He'd lit a bonfire.

So what was she supposed to do now? She couldn't very well attack the man. He was here doing her a favor. And not even a favor for her. He had a whole other life, and he probably had a girlfriend. Sure, he had a girlfriend. A man like him wouldn't be single and free. No way.

So where did that leave her?

She closed her eyes, plugged her nose and slipped down until she was completely immersed. Holding her breath, she waited, and waited, then she popped up again, desperate for air.

She sat up and reached for the soap and washcloth, but didn't use it. Instead, she wondered if she still had that vibrator she'd gotten as a gag gift at her wedding shower. It was still in the original package. Maybe now would be a good time to take it for a spin.

She blushed at the thought, then started washing, starting with her toes and working her way up. By the time she reached her face, she'd made peace with herself. She had needs. She had desires. It was perfectly natural. But she must remember not to jump on the nice man downstairs. Even if he was bought and paid for.

THE KIDS HAD GATHERED in the kitchen. They'd missed their normal dinner hour, and things were about to get ugly if Beth didn't do something about it soon.

She waited, though, because Jarred hadn't come out of the bathroom yet. It occurred to her that he might have fallen asleep in the tub. After all, she'd finished her bath, dried her hair, gotten dressed and even put on makeup.

"Where is he?"

She frowned down at Karen. "What have I said about whining?"

"That it's attractive."

"Unattractive."

"Unattractive," Karen repeated. "But it's only us. Why can't I be unattractive here?"

"Because we're not just family. We're also human beings who deserve to be treated as nicely as guests."

"Caleb's not a human being," Karen muttered.

Debbi giggled. "Yeah. He's dark matter from the underworld."

"Pardon me?" Beth asked.

Caleb sighed wearily. "It's from those stupid Galaxy Man comic books. Ignore them. They're dweebs."

"We are not," Debbi said. "You're the dweeb."

"Am not," Caleb shot back.

"Are, too."

"Am not."

"Are, too, infinity," Debbi shouted.

"Whoa, what's this? World War III?"

They all turned toward the door, toward Jarred. He stood like some Greek god, so big he blocked out the hallway behind him.

"We're not dweebs, are we, Jarred?" Karen asked.

"I don't believe so," Jarred said. "I've seen dweebs. Ugly little things. Hairy legs, long pointy noses. Nope," he said as he walked into the room. "No dweebs here."

"See," Debbi said, sticking out her tongue at her brother.

"You're so lame," Caleb muttered.

Beth wasn't sure if he meant his sister or Jarred.

Time for some intervention before things got out of hand. "Okay. What do you want on your pizza?"

"Pepperoni!"

"Sausage!"

"Pineapple!"

Beth grimaced. It was always the same, and she always ended up making a pizza with four distinct sections. She looked at Jarred. "What about you?"

"I don't care," he said. "Whatever you order is fine."

"Order?"

He nodded.

"You must be thinking about some other family. In this house, we make our pizza, right, kids?"

"Yeah!" Debbi said.

Jarred's brows came down sharply and he gave her an odd, confused look. "You're going to cook? Tonight?"

Beth smiled brightly, even though the thought of making dinner made her want to weep, she was so sore and tired. "Of course."

"Oh, no," he said. "Not tonight. Tonight, we go out to dinner."

Debbi and Karen leapt up as if Jarred had just offered them trips to the moon. "Can we, Mom?" Karen pleaded.

"Please, please, please?"

Beth looked at Jarred. "See what you've done?"

"Yep," he said. "Now, go on and get your purse." He paused. "You have a car?"

She nodded. "It gives basic transportation a bad name, but yes, I do have a car."

"Great. Let's saddle up and head on into town. Tonight's on me."

"Jarred," Beth said, raising her voice above the giggles and shrieks of her daughters. "You don't have to."

"Of course I do. So stop arguing, and let's get rolling."

Beth smiled, grateful to him for making it so easy to say yes. She got her purse from the counter, and by the time she turned, the girls were already at the back door, halfway outside. Caleb, however, was still sitting at the table. "Come on, honey," she said.

"I don't want to go."

"Sure you do. I know you're hungry."

"I'll make a sandwich."

"Caleb, when's the last time I let you stay here when the rest of us went to town?"

He stared hard at the tabletop. "Never."

"So what are the odds that I'll let you stay tonight?"

He looked up, glared at her for a solid ten seconds, then stood and shuffled toward the door. "I'll go," he said under his breath, "but I won't like it."

"Who knows?" Beth whispered in his ear. "You might actually have a good time."

"I won't," he said.

"Well, at least you'll get fed."

Caleb grunted. Then Jarred came up behind her. As she walked out the door, he put his hand on the small of her back. A light touch, not pushing, not groping. The hand of a gentleman.

What happened to her body wasn't ladylike, though. In fact, she debated running upstairs and putting on a sweater. The cotton bra and beige T-shirt she had on were completely inefficient at hiding her suddenly erect nipples.

But his hand kept up the pressure, and the door shut behind them. She looked down again. No way. No way would she let him see what he did to her. Especially not in front of her children.

She stepped aside, missing his hand instantly, and held up a finger. "I forgot something," she said. "I'll be right back."

She flung open the door, sprinted into the house and up to her room. She found a thick blue sweatshirt. It wasn't particularly attractive, but it would do an excellent job of hiding her predicament.

As fast as she could, she changed shirts, then hurried downstairs. Jarred stood at the door, holding it open for her. He blinked several times at her sweatshirt. She just gave him an enigmatic smile.

As she passed him on her way to the car, he leaned down and whispered, "I'm flattered."

She whipped around to face him. "What?"

His air of smug satisfaction made her want to smack him. "I said, I'm flattered."

"About what?"

He nodded toward her shirt.

"You're flattered because I had a stain on my shirt?"

His grin faltered, then held. "That's not why you changed."

"No?" She didn't give an inch. She just looked at him as if he were the most presumptuous person in Wyoming. "Why do *you* think I changed?"

He opened his mouth to speak, then hesitated. He opened it again, only to balk once more. Then he sighed, shook his head and traded smug for disappointment. "Never mind. I was mistaken."

"Okay," she said, turning to head for the car. But she didn't feel very victorious. Especially when he didn't touch the small of her back again.

CHAPTER SIX

"I'LL HAVE THE STEAK," Jarred said, looking at his menu. "Baked potato with everything."

"Excellent choice."

He looked up at the young waitress. She'd been flirting with him since she'd given them water and menus. Normally, he wouldn't have minded. She was pretty in her own way. Tall, dark hair up in a ponytail, and a voluptuous figure. But he didn't want her flirting so blatantly in front of Beth. And the children, of course. He hadn't given her any encouragement, not even a smile, but that didn't seem to matter.

"Soup or salad?"

"I'll have the soup," he said, with as little enthusiasm as he could.

"Potato, bean or split pea?" She said the words as if his answer would solve the riddle of the century.

"Split pea."

"Very good, sir."

The waitress walked away, sashaying so her bottom swayed like a metronome. Jarred looked over at Beth, who was frowning as she watched the waitress. "So, how's your back?"

Beth's gaze moved to him. For a long moment, she didn't say anything. She just looked him over, her frown deepening with every tick of the clock. "It's peachy," she said finally.

It wasn't the response he'd been hoping for. "You're a lot stronger than me. I'm sore from top to bottom."

The twins broke up laughing. He looked at them, tried to figure out what was so funny, then concluded it was some private joke.

"Girls, sit up straight, please," Beth said.

They quieted down immediately, but just as they had from the moment they'd gotten in the car, they stared at him. Really stared, as if they were waiting for him to turn into a bug or something. It was unsettling. Caleb, on the other hand, didn't stare. He avoided Jarred's glance as if a look would turn him to stone. And Beth? He never should have made that stupid remark about her shirt.

He'd been so sure! He'd seen her nipples stand up and salute, dammit. And then she'd come down in that bulky sweatshirt. But when she'd practically gelded him with that stare of hers, he realized he'd been completely off track.

"Jarred."

He focused on Beth. "Yes?"

"Why don't you tell us about Houston."

He nodded. He could do this. It was stupid to think about the other—nothing he could do about it, anyway. He had a home and a business to get back to. "It's hot," he said. "Humid. In the summer it's only fit for alligators and insects."

The girls giggled again, and he saw Beth's shoulders relax. He let out a breath and settled back himself. The tension had passed, and he was grateful for that.

"Why do you stay?"

"Because of the winters," he said. "They're short,

I'll admit that, and there are very few days that construction has to stop because of weather."

"I see," Beth said. "How big is your company?"

"I have eighty-four people on the payroll. We usually run four jobs at a time. Mostly single-family homes, but sometimes we do apartment buildings or offices."

"Wow, I'm impressed."

"Thank you," he said, letting the compliment sink in. He was fiercely proud of his company. He'd started from nothing, and now he was worth a couple of million. Not bad for an orphan.

"Do you still do construction work?"

He shook his head. "Not for a long time now. I have several foremen who oversee the actual jobs. I'm more of an administrator now."

"Do you like it?" Beth leaned forward, listening intently. He couldn't help but admire her intelligent eyes.

"Sure," he said automatically. But that wasn't entirely true, was it? "I like the results," he said. "The money's good, it keeps me busy."

"But?"

He shook his head, not at all surprised that she'd caught him in his half truth. "But the challenge isn't there anymore."

"I see," she said again.

The funny thing was, he knew she understood exactly what he meant, without further explanation. How about that.

"You're the kind of man who needs a challenge," she suggested. "New conquests, worthy foes."

He nodded. "But there isn't much money in tilting at windmills."

"Money isn't everything," she said softly.

"It buys security. With enough money, no one can touch you."

"That's not true at all. Money can't protect you from a broken heart."

"No, but staying away from involvement can."

Beth sat back as if he'd slapped her. The look of surprise on her face made him want to take back his words. "I meant—"

"I know what you meant," she said, turning from his gaze. "I don't agree with it, but I understand it."

The waitress came back carrying a round tray with their food on it. She put the tray on the table across from theirs and served Jarred his soup. Then, after a meaningful glance, she served the children. Finally, almost as an afterthought, she gave Beth her salad.

"Mom!" Debbi said, her voice in a panic.

Jarred looked at her, sure she'd hurt herself somehow, or even worse.

Beth reached across the table and took the sliced cucumbers off the girl's salad and put them on her bread plate. "Okay?"

Debbi relaxed and smiled happily, grabbed her fork and dug into her lettuce.

"We don't care for cucumbers," Beth whispered. "But the crisis has passed."

"Deftly handled," he said.

"Years of involvement," she said.

He smiled. And kept his mouth shut.

BETH FELT TERRIBLE. She had no business judging Jarred's life. It wasn't as if she was any paragon of virtue. Besides, there was a lot to be said for a policy of noninvolvement. Hadn't she decided to adopt just that? She'd made a horrible mess of her own life, choosing a man who couldn't, or wouldn't, take responsibility for his family. Now her concentration was solely on her children. Making a living, keeping them safe, easing the transition to a single-parent home.

The awful truth was, Jarred's comment had stung because somewhere in her obviously addled brain, she'd hoped... For what? Marriage? Oh, please. Even she couldn't be that insane. Not after what she'd been through, and knowing Jarred for exactly one day? But if not marriage, if not *involvement,* what did she want?

Sex.

She coughed, nearly choking on the piece of lettuce in her mouth.

Everyone looked concerned as she cleared her throat and wiped her eyes. Just seeing the trace of mascara on her napkin made her feel ludicrous. She'd put on makeup for Jarred. She'd switched shirts to hide her reaction to him, then lied straight-faced. Now she was upset because he didn't want to marry her, which wasn't what she wanted, anyway. But how on earth could she want sex with a total stranger?

If there was a bigger fool in Wyoming, she'd eat her napkin.

"Are you okay?" Jarred asked, his concern genuine, if she could believe his voice.

"Oh, yeah. I'm just fine. Just swell."

He looked at her crookedly, and she took another bite of salad, hoping he'd lose interest.

"Beth?"

Damn. "Yes?" she said after swallowing. It wouldn't be good for the children to see their mother get the Heimlich maneuver the first time they visited the town diner.

"I..." He stopped, stared hard at his soup for a moment, then looked back at her. "Tomorrow we'll clear out the plaster," he said. "And then I want to start on the roof. While I'm doing that, you can fix up the holes we left today."

"Great!" Beth said, too enthusiastically if the baffled look Caleb gave her was any indication.

"I'd like to stop at the General Store on the way home. Pick up a few things if it's still open."

"Sure," she said. "No problem."

"Including some liniment," Jarred continued. When she wrinkled her nose, he smiled. "Don't worry. I'll get the nonsmelly kind. It works just as well."

"I didn't know they made nonsmelly liniment."

"Yeah. They do."

"Oh, okay then."

Caleb continued to look at her with troubled eyes. He didn't understand the tone of the conversation, and frankly, neither did she. Something was going on. Something that had everything to do with hormones and nothing to do with the sense God gave a rabbit. Jarred just befuddled her. In a way that was completely new. She didn't understand him, and she sure as shootin' didn't understand herself.

The best thing to do, she decided, was keep her mouth shut. Finish dinner, go to the store, go home, then lock herself in her room.

That decision made, she didn't even mind when the waitress came and fawned all over Jarred. Well, she didn't mind *much*.

THEY WALKED ACROSS the street from the Main Street Grill to the General Store. Beth glanced over at Twyla's Tease 'n' Tweeze and thought about making an appointment. Not just for a haircut, but for the whole nine yards. Manicure. Pedicure. Massage. Facial.

Yeah, she'd make that appointment the very moment she won the lottery. If there was a lottery in Wyoming. Just her luck, there wouldn't be.

"Tell you what, ladies," Jarred said. "Caleb and I will meet you here in a half hour. We have some guy things to buy."

Beth's gaze shot over to her son. He looked as if he was going to bolt. Surely, he'd refuse to go. But then he glanced over at her and she pleaded with her eyes. He could be so sweet when he wanted to. He just hadn't wanted to in a long time.

He grunted, stuck his hands in his pockets and shuffled off after Jarred.

"Can't we go with them?" Karen asked.

"No. Jarred wants to spend a little time with Caleb."

"Oh, man," Debbi said, kicking at a rock.

"Tell you what, though. I bet they have a new shipment of Galaxy Man comics inside. You can go have a look at them. Just let Jarred have some time with Caleb."

She'd obviously said the magic words. The girls took off so fast, Beth had to yell out for them to slow down.

Beth didn't hurry to go inside. She let the cool evening air wash over her as she looked around, trying to adjust to the fact that Lightning Creek was her town now. Her home. If things went well, it would be her last home. It was a good place to raise children. Clean air, clean water and all the scenery a person could ask for. Even here, on Main Street, things were quaint and pretty. There was a railed boardwalk lining the wide boulevard, and the buildings all had that small-town feel. The statue of the bronc rider was her favorite, though. Right smack dab at the intersection of Main Street and Pine, the homage to cowboys said more about the town than any brochure.

Across the way, Reilly's Feed Store was having a sale on saddle polish and alfalfa. Not exactly big-ticket items back in San Diego. And then there was Twyla's beauty shop—decorated like something out of *The Wizard of Oz,* ruby slippers and all.

As she walked through the door of the General Store, she saw a poster for a local rodeo, and a hand-lettered sign advertising free kittens. Better hope the kids didn't see that one. Eventually, when the house was finished, she'd think about a pet. A dog. She'd like that. But not yet. Not when she could barely feed her human dependents, let alone additional critters.

She didn't really need anything. She'd done her shopping for the week already. But the store carried so much, she normally liked to wander around. Not tonight. Tonight she'd just go look at the books and check up on the girls. She glanced over at Jarred and Caleb, wondering how they were getting along, and if Caleb was being nice.

Jarred could be a good influence on Caleb, if only her son would listen. On the other hand, she didn't want the boy becoming too attached, just to have another man in his life take off and not look back.

They stood by the tools, and Jarred was saying something that interested her son. She could see it in his stance. For the moment, the hunched shoulders were gone, his hands weren't shoved deep in his pockets, and his gaze wasn't fixed on the ground. She smiled and looked away, afraid to break the spell Jarred had created. She trusted him. For the most part, that is.

"Mom, look!"

She heard Karen's voice just as she hit the book-and-magazine section. Karen had a comic book in each hand and was waving them like flags.

"Don't!" Debbi said, her voice elongating the word into a singsong plea.

"Why not?"

"*Because!*" Debbi insisted, holding her sister steady, looking her straight in the eyes.

Karen fought to break free, but only for a moment. Some lightbulb went on and she smiled widely, then brought the comic books up to her chest and crossed her arms over them.

If Beth didn't know better, she'd think the girls were trying to buy *Playboy*s instead of Galaxy Man, they were so intent on hiding the covers from her. But Beth had been their mother too long to get in a lather about their comic books, or their secrets. If it was important, she'd find out about it sooner or later.

She perused the cooking magazines, then shifted to the home decor section. Everything looked like too much work, so she moved over to the books. Mysteries, romance novels, thrillers. When was the last time she'd sat down with a good book and read the whole thing from start to finish? Heck, when had she last finished a book at all?

In her old life, she'd found such solace and companionship in her books. In this life, there wasn't time for anything so ethereal. Oh, what the hell. She'd find the time.

Her decision was a quick one because Nora Roberts had a new book out. She grabbed it before she changed her mind. "Okay, kids. Let's go check out."

She herded the girls to the counter and paid for their goodies. Then she saw Jarred and Caleb walking toward them. If she hadn't seen it with her own two eyes, she wouldn't have believed it: Jarred had his arm on Caleb's shoulder, and Caleb was smiling! It was a small miracle, but a miracle nonetheless.

"PLEASE, JARRED!"

"Pretty please!"

Jarred knew there was no way he was going to talk himself out of this mess. The twins had him by the arms, tugging him up the stairs, begging him to tell them a bedtime story. He wouldn't have minded so much if he knew any stories, but he didn't. Not even one.

"Pretty please with sugar on top," Debbi pleaded.

"With sugar and a cherry?" Karen added

"With sugar and a cherry and sprinkles?" Debbi countered.

"All right," he said, hoping they'd let go of his arms. No such luck. They just pulled harder. What he wanted to know was whose idea was it to give this much energy to six-year-olds? A sadist, that's for sure.

They reached the landing, and then he was rushed to the girls' bedroom. They were already in pajamas. Galaxy Man was the theme, and it was obviously a favorite, because they had Galaxy Man sheets and comforters on their twin beds.

Debbi scurried under the sheets and lay down, her big green eyes wide-awake and waiting. Great.

He found a chair, a very small chair that he hoped was stronger than it looked, and sat down. He felt as if his knees could scrape his chin. But he'd only be here a few minutes, right?

"Galaxy Man," Debbi stated.

"Galaxy Man when he met the dark forces for the first time," Karen added.

He didn't know very much about the superhero. But how different could he be from Batman or Superman? Jarred had read those comics as a kid. "Okay, one story. Then sleep," he said.

Karen shook her head. "No, two."

He shook his head right back. "No, one."

She scrunched up her face. "All right."

He began his story, pulling in a bit of Batman, a bit of Superman, some Green Lantern and some Popeye for good measure. He wasn't sure Galaxy Man needed spinach, but tonight he had two cans worth.

The girls didn't stop him, even when he was sure they'd caught on to his mixed-up tale. They just lay there, spellbound, watching him so closely he automatically started mugging for them. He was no actor, but for the twins he went all out. He used a scary voice for Ming from the planet Ork. A high falsetto for his heroine, Miss Lauren Bacall from the planet Bogart. Galaxy Man saved the two little girls, who just happened to be named Debbi and Karen. And after slipping from the clutches of the evil Mr. Ed, the Talking Horse of Doom, Galaxy Man, Lauren and the twins made a nice home for themselves in Palm Springs, including an indoor-outdoor pool and central air.

By the time Galaxy Man had saved the world, the real Debbi and Karen were struggling to stay awake. They kept closing their eyes, then opening them, only to have them flutter closed again.

"More," Debbi whispered.

"Tomorrow," he whispered back.

Two pairs of eyes closed a final time, and Jarred stood up. He had to bite his lip not to yell, the pain in his back was so acute. He'd been a jerk for sitting in that little chair after the kind of day he'd had. He rubbed his lower back, trying to ease the kink, and then he felt another hand next to his.

He started to turn, but Beth whispered, "Sh. Just be still."

He obeyed, letting his own hand drop as she massaged the small of his back. She sure knew how to use her hands. The feeling was indescribably wonderful. He closed his eyes, surrendering to the bliss. He moaned, and Debbi rolled over.

"Come on," Beth said, stilling her hand. "Let's get out of here before we wake them."

He followed her like a puppy. He'd roll over and play dead if she'd only rub his back some more.

She led him to the attic stairs, which were so low he had to crouch down almost double, and up into the room that was his for the night. She'd made up a futon bed for him that looked reasonably comfortable and had set out a stack of clean towels. Even his bag had been brought up.

"Lie down," she said.

He wanted to. Lord, he wanted to. But instead, he turned around and put his hands on her shoulders. "I'm okay," he said. "I'm worried about you, though."

"I'm a little sore," she admitted.

"A little sore," he repeated. "Right. Like Hurricane Andrew was a little windy."

She moved her head in a slow circle from one side to the other. "Okay, so I'm a lot sore," she admitted.

"You know where that bag is? The one from the store?"

She pointed to his suitcase, and he saw the bag right behind it.

"I don't think we should do this here," he said.

"No?"

He got the new tube of vanilla-scented soothing rub and shook his head. "I think we need to do this in your bedroom."

"Oh?" she asked, both brows raised.

He nodded. "I'm going to make you feel so good, you're going to offer me your firstborn."

"You can have him," she said, smiling wryly.

"You won't be such a smart-ass when I get through with you."

"Is that a threat?"

He smiled right back at her. "It's a promise."

CHAPTER SEVEN

BETH SAW THE MISCHIEF in Jarred's eyes and realized two things: one, she should excuse herself this second, run to her room and lock the door behind her, and two, she wasn't going to listen to the first thing.

"A promise?" she repeated, liking every one of the possibilities that flitted through her mind.

He nodded, his gaze unwavering and dangerous.

She nodded, her senses nearing overload. To have a man want her so blatantly, and such a man! He could have all the twenty-year-old secretaries he wanted, for heaven's sake. It had been so long, too long, since she'd felt the least bit desirable. Dan had seen to that. But she must be somewhat appealing, right? To cause that look in Jarred's eyes?

She felt his hand take hers, swallowing it whole, and then he led her to the stairs, bending low so he wouldn't hit the ceiling. She didn't even have to duck.

He kept on pulling her forward, leading her straight into temptation. She left her last vestige of good sense in the hall as they walked through the door to her room.

Jarred stopped when he reached the bed. He let go of her hand as he captured her gaze. She felt his rough finger brush her right cheek in a tender caress that stole her breath. "Lie down," he said, his voice whisper soft yet thick as a growl.

"Okay," she said, letting herself drop on her back, arms stretched out as if she were falling into a pool.

He chuckled, a deep, sensual sound, and then she felt the bed dip as he sat down next to her. "I think this will work better if you turn over. You might also consider using the pillow."

She nodded. Without a moment's hesitation, she turned over and crawled sideways until she found her pillow in her hands. Then she flopped down again.

"Good girl," he said.

She smiled happily, closed her eyes and waited for whatever was going to happen to happen.

He didn't keep her in suspense long. The bed moved under his weight, and then she felt him beside her. His leg went over her backside until he straddled her. She felt his knees touch her hips. That's all. Just his knees.

Then she heard a scratching sound, and it took her a minute to realize he was rubbing his hands together. She grinned, thinking of a hungry man about to attack a delicious meal. Only she was the entrée.

When his hand touched her lower back, sneaking underneath her sweatshirt, the image fell apart. He hadn't been rubbing his hands in glee, only trying to make them warmer. Which was a lovely thing to do, even if it wasn't quite as salacious as she'd hoped for.

Her giggle stopped his hands, and she cut the sound off instantly, afraid that she'd given him the wrong impression.

When his hands moved up, she vowed to keep silent—well, maybe keep it down to simple moans of pleasure.

His warm palms moved up her back until he

reached her bra strap. A second later, that barrier was unlatched, and he was pushing aside the material.

"Oh my goodness," she whispered.

"I haven't started yet."

All she could do was sigh. It was like some wonderful dream. Not even her dream. She'd never have dared imagine this scenario, or her part in it. Not in a million years.

She was a good girl. Always had been. She'd waited until marriage to sleep with Dan, and had never thought of going outside the marriage, even in the worst of times. The whole concept of making love with a man she barely knew had never appealed to her...before. But now, it was too easy to see the appeal.

Jarred was only here for one night, maybe two. Then he'd fly back to his real life, never to be seen again. No entanglements. No expectations—well, except for the one. No promises to break, no involvement.

Why not? Why not abandon her body to this stolen pleasure? When was the last time she'd done anything solely for herself? She smiled, remembering that just a few hours ago, she'd thought the height of decadence was a facial and a pedicure.

His hands slipped from her skin, and then she heard them rub together again, only this time, the scratch of skin on skin was replaced by the succulent sound of cream between his palms. She readied herself for his touch, willing the last of her reservations to take a hike, and sighed deliriously when his hands found her once more.

Deeply, powerfully, he massaged her back, paying special attention to her shoulders, even though he had to fight her sweatshirt. The sweet scent of vanilla wafted over the bed, making her feel more like a dessert than an entrée.

"Wait," she said.

His hands stilled.

She reached both hands over her shoulders and grabbed the thick material, drawing it up until the back of the sweatshirt was bunched at her neck. Not brave enough to just sit up and let him see the whole enchilada, she pulled the material over her head, keeping the front tucked around her breasts. It took another few seconds to get comfy again, and Jarred waited patiently. As soon as she was settled, though, he continued his magic.

It was even better now that the shirt was out of the way. Nothing obstructed the long strokes, the power of his hands or the way he knew instinctively where she needed the most kneading. Just to feel his very human touch was almost more than she could stand. Her body soaked it up like a sponge, sending pleasure signals to her brain in wave after wave of bliss.

"This is heaven," she whispered.

"I told you so."

"No you didn't. You said I'd feel good. This makes mincemeat out of good."

He chuckled again. "My pleasure, ma'am. It's all part of the service."

"Well, it's one heck of a service."

Then he concentrated on her right shoulder blade, and she couldn't talk anymore.

JARRED LISTENED to her moan as he ministered to her lower back. The longer he rubbed, the deeper into trouble he got.

Why'd she have to lift her sweatshirt like that? Wasn't it torture enough to have her lying on the bed like a rag doll? Or to hear her contented purr?

He should have his head examined.

What had he been thinking? That she was some good-time girl out for a fling? She was a mother, dammit. A woman in the middle of a divorce. Of *course* she was vulnerable. He'd seen that from the get-go.

So why had he led her down here? Why was he on top of her, so aroused he didn't know whether to yell or go blind? He should have stopped this before it began. At least stopped it before he'd felt the softest skin in the world. Now he didn't know if he *could* stop. Not until he'd...

"Oh, yes," she whispered.

Oh, no, he thought. She was going to move. She was going to turn over, and if she turned over, he was a complete goner. One look at those breasts he'd been imagining for the last hour and he'd go crazy.

He stilled his hands, wanting to go on, desperate to go on. But he couldn't. Not with her. Not like this.

He'd come here to assuage his guilt, not add to it.

Before he could change his mind, before she moved another inch, he brought his hands up and scrambled off the bed, careful not to touch her or even look at her.

"Jarred?"

The confusion in her voice almost made him stop, but he forced himself to hurry to the door.

"What...?"

He opened the door, willing himself not to look back. He tried to speak, but had to clear his throat first. "I'll, uh, see you in the morning," he said, his voice so gravelly he barely recognized it. "Good night."

He didn't wait for her to respond. He just got the hell out of her room and shut the door behind him. He thought about going up to his room and locking the door, but there was something he needed to do first. A shower. A really cold shower.

BETH STARED AT THE DOOR, waiting for him to open it again. For him to chuckle, to tell her he'd just been kidding. The seconds ticked by, and the door remained shut.

What the heck had just happened? She looked down at her bunched-up sweatshirt, her unclasped bra. And then the full impact of the mistake she'd made came crashing in like a tidal wave.

"Oh, no," she cried, putting her head in her hands. Humiliation burned her from the inside out, so powerful she thought she might burst into flames. She'd thought... She'd been so *sure*.

Was she that out of touch that she didn't even know the difference between teasing and flirting? Was she so filled with lust that she misread every innocent sign? What must he think of her? Oh, God, she felt like Mrs. Robinson trying to seduce Dustin Hoffman. Taking off her shirt in front of him like some...some harlot!

Please, she thought, *let him leave. Let him just go back to Houston tonight.* If he left now, before she saw him again, she had a chance of getting over this. But if he was still here in the morning...

She'd have to shoot herself.

Forcing herself out of bed, she shrugged out of her remaining clothes and put on the longest, dowdiest nightgown she owned. She barely looked at herself as she brushed her teeth and washed her face.

When she crawled into bed and turned out the light, she hugged her pillow close, wondering how she was ever going to sleep. She'd made a first-class fool of herself tonight, and she kept replaying her mistakes over and over. Each new thought ripped out another piece of her already-sagging confidence and sent it through the shredder.

The feel of him still lingered on her skin, in the warmth that penetrated and soothed even while she writhed in torment.

She'd failed at being a wife. And now she'd failed at being a woman.

BETH'S EYES OPENED. It was morning. Despite her acute misery, she had slept. Now she had to face the world. And unless her guardian angel had been paying attention last night, she had to face Jarred. She'd rather confront a firing squad.

No way she could get out of it. It was already six-thirty, and the kids would be up any minute clamoring for breakfast.

It didn't take her long to dress. She didn't bother to shower, knowing the kind of day she had ahead of her. No longer caring what she wore, she grabbed an old T-shirt and her overalls. They made her look like Ma Kettle, but so what?

Dressed, face washed, hair as brushed as it ever got, teeth cleaned, she stood at her door, knowing she'd used up all her diversions. She had to face the day.

Taking a deep breath, she left her room and headed for the kitchen. A strange odor caught her attention the moment she stepped off the stairs. By the time she was halfway to the kitchen she knew what it was. Coffee.

But her kids didn't know how to make coffee.

She turned the corner and saw that her kids weren't even awake. Jarred was.

He stood at her stove, a spatula in one hand, a steaming cup of coffee in the other, looking sinfully handsome in his jeans and a pale blue polo shirt that matched his eyes. The Bisquick was out, the table was set with plates and cutlery and napkins and glasses and both milk and juice. Her mouth fell open as her gaze moved back to Jarred and she watched him flip a pancake.

"Morning," he said, as if nothing at all had happened last night. As if she hadn't been the most colossal idiot in the Western Hemisphere.

"What's this?"

"Breakfast."

"But...?"

He turned, giving her a generous smile. "How do you like your coffee? Or would you like orange juice first?"

Utterly stunned, she opened her mouth, but instead of saying "Cream and Sweet'n Low," she just started sobbing. Big sobs. Huge, shoulder-racking sobs. The tears filled her eyes and spilled down her cheeks, and there was nothing at all that she could do about it.

"What the hell?" Jarred threw the spatula on the counter and rushed over to her. "What happened?"

He looked so panicked, it made her cry harder. She turned away, not wanting him to see her like this, willing herself to stop, to get a grip, but nothing worked. Months, years of frustration and anger poured out of her, and she was helpless to stem the tide.

"God, Beth, what's wrong?" Jarred put his arm around her, and although she hesitated, he pulled her close, right up to his chest. Abandoning the last shred of her dignity, she leaned against his strong body and grasped his shirt in both hands as she buried her wet face against his chest.

"Sh," he whispered. "It's okay. We don't have to have pancakes. I can make something else."

She laughed, right in the middle of sobbing. Hiccuping twice, she took in a jagged breath, groaned, then hiccuped again. But at least the crying stopped.

His hands were on her back, holding her close, rocking her back and forth, comforting her as if she were a child. Which is just what she felt like. A foolish child who couldn't control her emotions, who mistook kindness for a come-on. She let go of his shirt and stepped back, too tired of being humiliated to be humiliated.

"What happened?"

"The coffee," she said, her voice choked with emotion. She felt herself wanting to let loose again, but used all her strength to control herself.

"I thought you liked coffee," he said.

"I do. I like pancakes, too."

He just looked at her, his head crooked to the side like a confused beagle. How could she explain herself? Or at least dissuade him from thinking she'd gone insane.

"It's just that you're the first person since my mother—" She had to stop and swallow until she could speak again. "You're the first person to make me breakfast," she said.

"Ever?"

She nodded.

"Your husband?"

"Never even made coffee. Not for me."

"Well," Jarred said, frowning. "Then he was a jackass."

She laughed, which felt very good. Finally, she could feel her feet under her again, and she was even able to grab a paper towel from the counter to wipe her face. "Yeah, he was," she said.

"So how'd a bright girl like you end up with a donkey like him?"

Beth shook her head. "It's a long and sad story."

"I've got all morning."

"No you don't. You need to turn those burning hotcakes."

He whirled around to grab the spatula, but one pancake didn't make it. He tossed it in the sink, put more butter in the pan and spooned out another.

Beth watched him for a long while, amazed at his ease in her kitchen. At the casual way he cooked, not making a bit of fuss. She thought about Dan. He'd always said his woman should be barefoot and pregnant while she cooked dinner. He'd tried to make it sound like a joke, but it wasn't funny. Maybe that wasn't fair. He hadn't known any better. "He wasn't a complete jerk," she said.

Jarred turned around again. "No?"

She shook her head. "No. He could be really sweet. He had some old-fashioned ideas about marriage, but that wasn't his fault. He got it from his parents."

Jarred nodded. "Yeah, I could see where that could happen."

"I mean," she continued, "it wasn't such a big deal, him not making coffee. I didn't mind."

"I'm sure you didn't," Jarred said, his voice deceptively calm. "But it was his loss. He never got to see a smile like the one on your face when you walked into the kitchen."

She lowered her gaze, not sure what to say, how to feel. He was being so nice to her, which didn't make sense after what she'd done last night.

"Listen," he said, turning to the stove once more. "Change of plans. At least for me. I'm going to work on the roof today. If I hustle, I can get it all done by tonight. I went out this morning and took a look. It's not as bad as I first thought."

"Isn't that a two-person job?"

He shrugged. "It goes faster with two people, but—"

"Then I'll help."

"I don't know, Beth. I don't know that I want you up on the roof."

"Mom," a voice from the hallway interrupted. "Debbi won't stop using my towel."

Beth leaned toward the door. "Debbi, stop using Karen's towel." Then she turned back to Jarred. "We'll get to work right after breakfast," she said, letting him know the debate was over.

"We'll see," he said, in the exact same tone she used when she didn't want to come out and say "no way" to her kids.

Karen ran into the room, tears flowing, hair a blond shaggy mess, one tennis shoe on, the other foot bare. "She won't stop."

Beth smiled. "Look at the table."

Karen sniffed dramatically, but curiosity won out.

She saw the set table, Jarred at the stove, the big stack of pancakes waiting on the counter. Instantly, all her problems vanished as her eyes grew wide with wonder. "Jarred *cooked?*"

"Jarred did," Beth said.

"Men don't cook," another voice said. A sleepy nine-year-old-boy's voice. Caleb came into the kitchen, rubbing his half-opened eyes. He'd managed to dress, putting on his favorite *X-Files* T-shirt, but he hadn't washed his face yet.

"Sure they do," Jarred said.

"No they don't," Caleb shot back. "That's women's work."

"Women's work?" Jarred turned to the boy, holding his spatula like a shield. "Where'd you get that idea? There's no such thing as women's work. Well, except for having babies."

"That's not true," Caleb said as he went to his place at the table. "My father told me."

"Well, I'm sure your father is a very smart man, but I don't think he was up on his chefs."

"Huh?"

"Some of the greatest chefs in the world are men. Isn't that right, Beth?"

She nodded. "And some of the best roofers in the world are women. Isn't that right, Jarred?"

He narrowed his eyes at her. "That was a low blow."

She grinned, loving the feeling of winning for once, then sat down next to Caleb. She put her napkin on her lap, kissed her son smack on the lips, then turned to the chef. "I don't care for any orange juice. But I'll have my coffee with cream and Sweet'n Low, please. And four pancakes."

"Yes, ma'am."

CHAPTER EIGHT

JARRED PUT THE LAST of the pancakes down on the table and sat between the twins. Everyone seemed to like the breakfast, if the sounds of chewing and the lack of conversation were any indication. He couldn't cook much, just pancakes, omelets and spaghetti, but the years of taking care of himself had honed his skills. They were damn good flapjacks.

"Mrs. Oliver is going to pick you kids up after school," Beth said. "So right after breakfast, you run, don't walk, to your assorted bathrooms and get washed up. I want clean, shiny faces and brushed teeth for school today."

"Do we have to go to Mrs. Oliver's after school today?" Debbi asked, starting in on her second helping.

"I thought you wanted this play date. You begged me for it."

"That was before," Karen said, pouring enough syrup to fill a lake.

Beth gave her a look that even Jarred understood, and Karen stopped pouring. "Before what?" Beth asked.

"Before…" Karen looked at her twin.

"Before we had company," Debbi said.

Beth smiled enigmatically, moving her gaze to him. "That's very thoughtful, but Jarred has lots of work

today, so I'm sure he won't mind if you three play
with Melissa and Tony after school.''

"But—"

"No buts, Karen. Just finish your breakfast and go
clean up. I don't want you to be late for the bus.''

Both girls frowned deeply, although their crushing
disappointment didn't stop them from eating another
pancake each. Then Jarred took a look at Caleb. There
was trouble a-brewin' from that quarter, too.

"And what is your beef, young man?''

Beth had obviously also noticed the dark cloud
hanging over the table.

"Tony's a dork.''

"Then your visit is even more important. It's your
duty to teach him the real meaning of cool.''

Caleb didn't bother arguing. Smart kid. He'd never
win an argument with Beth.

Jarred took a long drink of milk, wondering how
in the hell he'd ended up in this family portrait. He
was used to standing alone, and even when he had
dated women with children, he'd never spent much
time with them. This was new territory, filled with
strange rituals and customs he didn't understand.

Beth was the biggest mystery of all. He still hadn't
recovered from the episode last night, let alone this
morning's crying jag. He'd been prepared for a cold
shoulder or a kick out the door for his behavior in her
room. He'd even planned out his apology, but it was
forgotten when she turned on the waterworks. What
kind of a man had she been married to? What kind
of father told a son that only women cooked?

Beth's admission that Dan wasn't a total jerk only
served to make Jarred like *her* better. He didn't know
the details, but he got the gist, and from where he sat,

Beth was better off without her ex, even if it meant tackling her new life by herself.

He'd get the roof done today. That way, he wouldn't worry about it raining or snowing. She'd still have a lot to do, but at least she'd have a solid roof over her head.

"Can I be excused?" Caleb asked, wiping his mouth with the back of his hand.

"*May* you be excused. Yes, you may," Beth said.

The boy shot up out of his chair as if he were escaping the demons of Hades and ran out of the room.

"Don't forget to brush your teeth," Beth called after him.

"Can we help Jarred clean up?" Debbi asked.

"Thank you for that nice offer," Beth said, "but you two need to get a move on. Besides, Jarred isn't cleaning up. I am."

Both girls groaned, but they behaved. They put down their napkins, climbed out of their chairs and headed for the stairs, looking back at Jarred longingly. It was cute as hell, but he still wasn't sure what they saw in him. He wasn't even sure what big girls saw in him, so why shouldn't he be clueless with the half-pint variety?

Beth stood up and started stacking the empty plates. "Thank you for the wonderful breakfast," she said. "It was really good."

"My pleasure."

She shook her head at him, and he saw a mirror image of his own confusion in her gaze. So she didn't understand him any better than he understood her. That helped, actually.

"Do you want another cup of coffee before you go?" she asked as she put the dishes in the sink.

"No, I'm fine." He stood up, taking the remaining pancakes with him to the counter.

"Hey, your job is done here. Go on, get out. You have a roof to fix. I'll be there as soon as I can."

"Are you sure?" Jarred waited for her to turn from the sink and look at him. "I don't mind helping."

"You've already done more than your share."

"Okay," he said, but he still didn't leave. He watched her do the simple chores. Clearing the table, wiping up spills. Putting the milk back in the refrigerator. And then she moved her arm in a particular way... and he remembered her naked back. The way she felt, so small and smooth and delicate beneath his rough hands. It was more than just a memory, though. It was visceral. The scent of vanilla suddenly filled the air, and his hands heated as if he'd just finished the massage.

"Is something wrong?"

He cleared his throat and his head at the same time, banishing the images, the scent, the touch. He backed up, heading toward the hallway. "No, just thinking. You know, the roof and stuff."

"Uh-huh."

"What are you smiling at?"

"If you were thinking about the roof, I'll eat a bug."

"Why do you say that?"

She leaned against the sink and crossed her arms over her baggy overalls. She shouldn't have looked good in them. They were too big, and they hid all the curves he knew firsthand were there. But she did look good. Too good.

"If I had to guess, I'd say you'd gone home. To the place you belong."

She'd seen *that* in his eyes? He didn't want to tell her she was wrong, and not because she'd ask what he was really thinking about. He simply didn't want to admit that he had a house in Houston, but he'd never felt as if he belonged there. He'd never felt he belonged anywhere.

"So I'm right, eh?"

He nodded. "On the money."

"I don't mention it much but, well… I'm a little psychic. Not much. But sometimes I'll know who's going to call just before the phone rings, or I'll wake up in the middle of the night, knowing somehow that one of the kids is sick. It's not anything I can count on, of course, but…" The word trailed off while her cheeks grew pink. "Anyway. Thanks for breakfast."

He had his own piece of psychic awareness. Beth was nervous. Now that the kids were gone and it was just the two of them, she didn't know what to do, so she was talking a mile a minute.

"You're welcome," he said. "Where can I find the ladder?"

"The side of the house, by the living room."

"Thanks." He turned to leave, and he heard her grateful sigh. She was right to be grateful that he was leaving. In fact, the only smart thing for him to do was get the work done and go home. It was too complicated here. Too confusing.

BETH CROUCHED ON THE ROOF, trying very hard not to look down. It wasn't a fear of heights that made her stomach tighten. It was the fear of sliding down the roof and bouncing on the ground below.

"Hand me that stack of shingles, would you?"

She lifted the pile on her right and slowly brought them over to Jarred. She put them down, then waited for him to need her again. But instead of taking the top shingle and hammering it into place, he paused, sat up on his haunches and lifted his polo shirt off.

It had gotten warmer, and he'd been working very hard, but still, did he have to do that? She gave in and let herself look him over. It was all she could do not to moan. What a chest. What a back. What a bod.

Broad, powerful shoulders, sculpted abs, clear tan skin and just exactly the right amount of chest hair.

Now he took the top shingle, bent forward, lined up the nail gun and let it fly. Like a well-oiled machine, he added one shingle after another, overlapping them perfectly, never making a mistake, never breaking from his rhythm.

All the while, she couldn't stop looking at his body. The way the muscles in his arms bunched and released. The way his slim stomach went in and out on each breath. The lock of hair that fell across his forehead.

Dear God, she was losing her grip. Not on the roof, but inside, where she kept her good sense. He made her feel things she had no business feeling. An ache between her legs, a tightness in her breasts. A yearning that made her mouth dry and her chest constrict.

"You okay?" He'd stopped, finished with the row. He was staring at her, and she had no idea for how long. "Beth?"

"Yeah?"

"You want to take a break?"

She shook her head.

"Sure? It's past one. Maybe get a little lunch?"

"I'm not hungry," she said absently, wishing he'd stop talking and start hammering.

"Well then, okay."

Then it hit her. "You're hungry!"

He grinned. "I could eat."

"Oh, I'm so sorry. I didn't... I meant..." She started to scramble over to the ladder, but she moved too fast and for a sickening second she thought she was a goner. But then his hand grabbed her upper arm and he pulled her back. He didn't stop until she was flush against him, her chest against his, her hands gripping the hard, hot steel of his shoulders.

She looked up. He could have let her go right then, and she wouldn't have fallen. The pull of his gaze was too strong. She felt frozen in time, in space. Acutely aware of his size and his closeness, and his state of undress, but none of those things mattered because it was his eyes that made her dizzier than any height.

His lips parted, and he lowered his head slowly. Agonizingly. Her own lips parted and her heart pumped furiously, the anticipation more than she could stand.

And then he kissed her. Gently at first. Just soft lips testing, teasing. Mapping out the terrain.

Her eyes fluttered closed as all her concentration went to her other senses. The masculine scent of heat and flesh. The feel of his tongue flicking against her lips. The taste of his essence as he abandoned all restraint and kissed her as if it were the last kiss in the world.

When she responded, meeting his tongue with her own in a swirling dance, he moved his arm behind her, snaking his hand into her hair. The power she felt in his arm, his hand, made her dizzy and faint, and she abandoned herself to his command, soaking in his desire for her as he whispered her name before plunging back into the sea of kisses.

Her hands moved across his shoulders, traversing each hill of flesh and muscle as a slow traveler, memorizing each contour. It seemed to her that she had more senses, more awareness than she'd ever had before; her focus was completely on his lips and completely on his scent and completely on the feel of him, and no sense was shortchanged.

When he moved his mouth down her chin, kissing, stealing licks along the way, he paused at her neck, then slid gracefully to the valley below her ear. Still holding her steady, he explored her sensitive skin, making her whole body tingle with goose bumps. He found her earlobe and nibbled, using his teeth and his tongue in a game of his own design. She moaned, unable to keep the pleasure contained even one moment more.

The hand at her waist moved down her back, his palm so wide and strong it made her feel like a baby bird, but when he slid over the hill of her buttocks, the sensation was quite human, all woman, all need.

"Beth," he whispered into her flesh, branding her forever. "This is crazy. I'm crazy. I want you so much."

She could only moan her agreement. It was crazy. Mad. Impetuous and dangerous. And she didn't care at all. The world could come to an end, and it wouldn't matter as long as she was in his arms.

No longer satisfied with her neck or her ear, he moved back to take her mouth once more.

High in their perch in the sky, miles from earth and

reality, she kissed him back with a passion she'd never known before. It was a completely new experience. One she'd never forget for the rest of her life.

This was enough. This was the thrill she'd been seeking last night. It was better than sex, better than consummation. The need and the denial as intoxicating as champagne. She'd never felt so alive.

Somewhere outside herself, she heard an engine. But it was down there, in the real world, and she let it go. But then she heard a man's voice. "Beth?" Sam's voice.

Jarred pulled back, his eyes wide with the realization of what he'd done. What they'd done. He moved his grip on her so she didn't fall, then helped her to the ladder.

He didn't say anything. Not a word.

She found her footing and started down, scary inch by inch, Jarred keeping a firm grip so she wouldn't fall. When she had gone down several steps, she looked up, right into his gaze. His smile.

She smiled back, then looked down again, ready to put her feet back on the ground.

CHAPTER NINE

"Looks like you've been busy."

Jarred shook Sam's hand. The older man's grip was as firm as ever, and Jarred could feel the calluses that were as much a part of Sam's personality as his easy smile. "It's a drop in the bucket," he said as Sam withdrew his hand and stuck it in his pocket. He'd seen Caleb do the same thing several times, and he wondered if the boy was imitating the man.

"Yep, it's gonna take a lot of work to get this place in shape."

Jarred started toward the house, where Beth had gone ahead to fix lunch. "It's too big a job for Beth, by herself. I mean, she's strong and capable, but this place…" He looked at the sagging porch, the boarded windows, the chipping paint. "This place needs a team of professionals."

"Beth'll do all right," Sam insisted. "It may take her a while, but she's pretty determined."

"I guess," Jarred said, even though he didn't really agree. Maybe she would get it all done, but it wouldn't be what the old house deserved.

"I'm just glad to see you're still here," Sam told him.

"Yeah, well, I couldn't go without doing something about the roof. I'd hate to see how bad it would be in real weather."

"How about we talk a minute before we head in for lunch?"

Jarred stopped, wondering if Sam had seen him kissing Beth on the roof. It shouldn't matter, but it did. Jarred didn't want Sam to think he was trying something slippery. He hadn't intended to kiss her, but she'd been so close, her heartbeat fluttering like wings, her eyes so wide and wanting....

"I wanted to thank you," Sam said, "for taking this on. And for coming back here at all."

Instantly, Jarred's mental image of Beth vanished and he was back with Sam, facing the man who'd given him so much. Who'd been there for him at the worst time in his life, when he'd needed a friend and a father figure. In return, Jarred had slapped him in the face. "I didn't come here for you," Jarred said, flustered at the emotion that sideswiped him. "I came here to get you out of my brain."

Sam laughed. "It's not the nicest compliment I've ever received, but it is heartfelt."

"I still feel awful about taking off like that. You were good to me, and I—"

"You have a chance to fix that now."

Jarred looked up at the roof. He'd be done by nightfall if he didn't take too much time for lunch. "I'm glad to do it."

"I wonder."

Jarred shifted his gaze to the older man. His stained, battered hat couldn't cover all his gray hair, and his shoulders were a bit hunched, but there was still a great deal of strength in Sam. He'd had a life built out of stone and sweat, and all he'd ever asked for was a good horse, a square meal and a kid to teach. Even though it had been years since their last real talk, Jarred knew the old cowboy was leading up to something. Something that Jarred wasn't going to like. "What do you mean, Sam?" he asked, knowing he was going to regret asking.

"I mean that while that check was very generous, and mighty appreciated, it still came up short."

Jarred tensed. "I gave you ten thousand dollars, Sam. If that doesn't cover what I owe, then I'm sorry."

Sam put his booted foot up on the porch and leaned his side against the rail. "I'm not asking for more money. Ten thousand covers that part of the debt nicely."

"That part of the debt?"

"The part about the car."

Now Jarred was confused. He hadn't taken anything else from the ranch except for a few clothes and about twenty bucks he'd won in a poker game. "I don't follow."

"You had a big loss in your life, son, I won't deny that. Losing your parents when you're a kid, well, that's just about the roughest break there is. You had some time to grow up before you left, but you didn't take advantage of that. I know you had your reasons, but the truth is, when you left that night, you showed me I hadn't done my job. I was responsible for taking a boy and making him into a man. I failed."

"That wasn't your fault. I was only sixteen."

"Sixteen is old enough to understand responsibility. It's old enough to care about people, and to do what's right."

"Okay, so I didn't know better back then. But I'm not sixteen anymore."

Sam laughed. "No, son, you're not. But I wonder.

Have you grown into the man I thought you'd become?"

Jarred looked away, his discomfort at talking about all this making him want to run. But of course, he couldn't do that. Not after telling Sam he wasn't a kid any longer. "I don't know, Sam. I think I'm doing okay."

"You ever been married?"

Jarred shook his head.

"Ever been close?"

Jarred shook his head again.

"But your company, it's doing fine?"

That was a question Jarred could answer with pride. "It's one of the largest independent construction companies in Houston."

"You must have a good staff. Good people to run things."

"I sure do. The best in the business."

Sam smiled. "Then it won't be too difficult for you to stay here awhile."

"What?"

"This house needs someone like you to see it through. This family needs someone they can count on."

"That would take months."

"Probably."

"I can't stay here that long. I have—"

"A business. So you've said."

"Look, Sam. I can't just drop my life and move out here to do charity work. I gave you the money I owed, plus a lot more. I've stayed an extra day so Beth would have a roof over her head. I can't do more than that."

"We'll see," Sam said, bringing his foot down. "We'll see if you're the man I'd hoped you'd be."

"That isn't fair."

"Fair? Fair ain't nothin' but a weather report, son, and you know that. You also know what's right. And what's cheatin'. And how to tell the difference."

Jarred opened his mouth to argue, to tell Sam that he'd gone off his rocker. But the stubborn mule took off for the door, leaving Jarred to kick at a rock and curse up a storm. No way was he going to stay here until this place was done. Especially after what happened on the roof. He had to get the hell away from here as fast as he could.

It took him a few minutes to cool down, but he did. Mostly out of necessity. He was hungry as hell, and the food was inside with Sam and Beth.

He went to the back door and let himself in.

"Everything's ready," Beth said. He could tell right off Sam hadn't told her about his idea. She looked too calm for that.

She and Sam stood at the sink while the old man rinsed his hands. Jarred looked at the spread she'd put out on the table. Bread, ham, cheese, and all the fixings. He spotted the big pitcher of iced tea on the counter, and he headed for that.

"Looks good enough to eat," Sam said, smiling at his little joke. "And so do you, Beth." He kissed her on the cheek, and she gave him a kiss in return.

"I look like hell and you know it, Sam," she said. "But thanks for lying."

"I don't lie. I may not see everything exactly as it is, but I never lie."

"Fair enough. Now let's eat."

Sam sat down just as Jarred brought the tea over,

taking the seat across from Sam. Beth took hers at the head of the table.

"Where are the kids?" Sam asked.

"At school. Then they're going to play at Mrs. Oliver's."

"I'm glad to know they're making friends. Doesn't surprise me, though. You have nice children, Beth."

"Thanks. I like to think so. Although I wish Caleb would…" She didn't finish the sentence, and Jarred had the feeling she didn't have time to say all the things she wished for her son.

"He's still waiting for his dad, eh?"

Beth nodded. She took some bread on her plate and set about preparing her sandwich. "I don't know what to do about it," she said. "I can't just tell him the truth."

Sam looked at her square on, his weathered face serious but kind. "He'll find out the truth whether you tell him or not. Kids are smart. They have a habit of catching on."

"I know," Beth said, reaching across to Sam's hand and giving it a squeeze. "But does he have to catch on so soon? I was hoping he'd find something here, something to care about. That would make it a lot easier."

"I don't think he can find anything until he's made peace with his daddy not coming for him. His door's shut tight."

Beth sighed. "How do you do it?" she asked. "You've helped so many boys. What's your secret?"

Sam's gaze went to Jarred, and he said, "I believe in them, even when I don't believe in the way they're acting. I talk to the goodness inside them, and somehow, they come around." The left corner of his mouth lifted in a wry grin. "Of course, with some it takes longer than others."

Jarred busied himself with his sandwich, spreading mayonnaise so hard he tore the bread. He wasn't going to listen. He wasn't going to let Sam Duncan manipulate him into doing something as crazy as staying here to fix the house. Hadn't he seen them kiss? Didn't he realize the kind of trouble that was brewing here?

Beth looked at him curiously, but he didn't let her get to him, either. He slapped another piece of bread on his sandwich and stood up. "I'd better get back to work if I'm going to finish by nightfall." He headed toward the door, purposely not looking back. He didn't want to see Sam's face.

"Son."

Damn. His hand was already on the door. Seconds from a clean getaway. He turned, as if facing a parent for punishment.

"I just wanted to tell you again that I think highly of you for coming out here. Some people would have just sent money. But you're putting in time, and trouble. That says a lot."

Jarred gave a quick glance at Beth. She was looking at him as if she thought he was nuts, or maybe just rude. But he wasn't going to explain. As far as he was concerned, this conversation with Sam was over and done with. "It was good seeing you again, Sam. I wish you well."

"You, too, son. I believe you'll do all right. I truly do."

Jarred nodded, then pushed open the door, getting out of there as quickly as he could. He had no illusions that Sam had taken back his request. The old coot wanted him to stay, to finish the house, to screw up his own business, mess up his life. Well, he wouldn't. He wouldn't!

He took a big bite of sandwich and chewed furiously. Ten thousand dollars was nothing to sneeze at, dammit. And he'd already worked here longer than he had to. Didn't that count for something?

It wasn't his fault Beth didn't have any help. He wasn't the one who'd left her and her kids. And it wasn't his fault that this old house was falling apart. He'd donated money to a worthy cause and come out here to do a good deed. And what did he get for his trouble? A kick in the ass.

Dammit, he wasn't going to let it get to him. He was going to finish the roof and get the hell out of here. Get away from Beth and her kids, and Wyoming, and memories, and mostly, he was going to get away from Sam. He'd paid his debt. He didn't owe anything more. And that was final.

BETH TURNED TO SAM. He still had his gaze on the door, but now he had a smile on his face. Not a big grin, but a secret smile, a knowing smile. "All right," she said. "What's going on?"

Sam shook his head slowly back and forth. Then he took another bite of his sandwich, finished that, and took another. Beth was just about ready to shout at him when he said, "Did he tell you how he came to Lost Springs?"

"No. He hasn't said much of anything personal."

Sam took a drink of tea, then put the glass down. He turned to Beth, his smile gone. "From what I was told, his folks had been well-to-do at one time. At least we think so. The car they'd been driving was a

Mercedes-Benz. The clothes they had in their suit-cases were pricey. From the outside, it looked like they were one big happy family.''

''And?''

''They left their son with a hotel maid in Casper. He was nine at the time. Then they went for a drive. The accident was so bad, it took a long time to figure out who they were. The authorities did a little dig-ging. Turns out the father was in debt. Heavy debt. They didn't own anything at all, except for that fancy car and the clothes they'd taken with them. There was nothing left for the boy, and that's how he came to me. Heartsick, confused, and as angry as a starving bear cub.''

''Oh, God, that's terrible. Was it really an acci-dent?''

Sam shrugged. ''No way to tell. No one else got hurt, though. The car just ran into a mountain. And that was it.''

''Jarred must have been devastated. His whole world was taken from him in an instant.''

''Yep. That's pretty much how it was. He hated the ranch. He hated the other boys. He hated life.''

Beth's heart constricted for the boy Jarred had been. So much pain. So like her own son, only Jarred's hurt had no end. ''Tell me something, Sam. Why did he come back here? Why did he volunteer for the auction?''

Sam gave her another of his enigmatic smiles. ''I think you should ask Jarred that one.''

She shook her head. ''You're not going to tell me, are you?''

''Nope.''

"And you're not going to tell me what you said that set him off today."

"Nope."

"You're as stubborn as they come, aren't you, Sam?"

"Yep."

Beth laughed, and so did her old friend. She'd never been close to him when she was a child. He'd been close to her grandfather, though. Sam had taken care of Lucas when he got sick, and he'd been there with her when her grandfather had died. Sam was the one who suggested she turn this place into a bed-and-breakfast. He was the one who had told her she had a place to come home to.

So she'd let him get away with his cryptic answers and his secret smiles. In time, she was sure, everything would come out. Jarred would tell her all she wanted to know. And in the telling, something good would happen. Because Sam said so.

BETH WAVED UNTIL SHE couldn't see Sam's pickup truck anymore. Just the cloud of dust that took its time settling back down to earth. She went to the side of the house, to the ladder. "Jarred," she called, looking up at the edge of the roof.

"Yeah?"

"Can you hold the ladder, please? I'm coming up."

His head appeared over the jagged ridge of shingles. "You don't have to. I've got things under control."

"I want to."

"That's okay. You just rest. I've got it."

"Don't be silly. It'll get done twice as fast if I help."

"All right," he said grudgingly. He took hold of the ladder, steadying it for her slow climb. When she got to the top, his strong arms pulled her to safety.

He turned away abruptly, going back to the row of shingles he'd been working on.

This wasn't exactly how she'd pictured things. Had he forgotten already how he'd held her in his arms? How his kisses had made her weak in the knees? How desire had made them both crazy?

Or had she gotten things wrong again?

No. This time, she wasn't going to doubt herself. He'd kissed her, and kissed her hard. She hadn't made that up. She'd seen the heat in his gaze and felt the need in his muscles.

Sam had said something to him. That's what happened. Sam had seen them kissing, and he'd given Jarred hell for it. She should have figured that out right away. "Jarred?"

"Yes?" He didn't look at her or even stop using the electric nail gun.

"I don't know what Sam said to you, but I want you to know I'm not sorry we kissed."

He stopped, jerking his head up so fast she thought he might lose his balance. "What?"

"I know Sam must have read you the riot act, but that's only because he thinks of me as a sort of surrogate granddaughter. I don't think he thinks of me as a...well, as a woman."

"He doesn't," Jarred said, not as a question, but as a slightly bewildered statement.

"I think he's just trying to protect me. That's all. He knows what I've been going through this past year. How hard it's been. He doesn't want me to get hurt.''

She waited for Jarred to say something. To stop staring at her like that. As if he couldn't understand a word she was saying.

''What I'm trying to say is that it's okay. You don't have to worry about it. I realize that things got a little out of hand, that's all. We kissed. No big deal. I...I mean, it was a big deal. I liked it. A lot. But it wasn't a big...deal.''

Jarred's eyes narrowed. His mouth turned down into a frown, which deepened into a scowl.

''I'm sorry,'' she said, her face heating with embarrassment. ''I didn't mean anything by that. I just didn't want you to feel—''

''Beth,'' he interrupted, his voice as sharp as a knife edge.

She stopped, leaned back and thought about dashing down the ladder, wondering if she could do it without killing herself.

''Dammit,'' he mumbled under his breath. ''Beth,'' he said again, ''I'm not leaving tonight or tomorrow night.''

''Oh?''

''I'm not leaving until the house is done. Okay? Happy now?''

She couldn't have been more shocked. He was going to stay until the house was done? But he had another life. A business to run. Oh, God, that meant he'd be here for months. Living here, under the same roof. Day after day after day.

''I'll call tonight. Have my things sent out here. Then I'll go over the plans for the house again, and I'll figure out what needs to be done.''

"You will?"

He nodded. "I'm not going to leave until the last coat of paint is dry. And that's final."

"I see," she said, finally coming out of her shocked stupor. Finally hearing everything he said. "I'd just like to know one thing."

"Yeah?"

"Who the hell invited you?"

CHAPTER TEN

JARRED'S FIRST THOUGHT was that he had his out. Beth didn't want him to stay, and it was her house. He should feel relieved, right? So how come he didn't? "Okay," he said, focusing on the roof instead of Beth's indignant expression. "Forget it. I'm sorry I said anything."

"That's it? Just forget it?"

"I made a mistake, that's all."

"Some mistake," she said.

He chanced a glance, and was immediately sorry. She looked hurt. Sad. So beautiful it made him want to kiss her all over again. He reached over to where she sat and touched her arm lightly. "Hey, I really am sorry. I didn't mean to upset you."

She met his gaze, hers still wounded, but not as badly as a moment ago. "I just think you should ask a person."

"You're right," he said, withdrawing his hand. Touching her wasn't such a good idea. "It's just that—"

"Yes?"

He shook his head, picked up the nail gun again, and finished up the shingle he'd been working on. "It's nothing."

She didn't push him. She didn't harp on his rudeness. She didn't even take him to task for talking to her so sharply. But she also didn't smile. And her glances were troubled, not filled with the sexual innuendo they'd had before Sam's visit. He figured that was for the best. The kiss had been a mistake. One he longed to make again, true. But he wouldn't. He'd finish the roof and go home. Forget about Beth and her kids and the house and Sam and the old debt that had been an albatross around his neck for years.

Beth handed him the next stack of shingles without him having to ask her. He worked quietly, focusing all his energy on finishing the job. Beth didn't say a word. She kept up with his pace, and she even positioned the shingles for him so all he had to do was nail them down.

They worked like that all afternoon. Quietly. Intensely. Sweating in the hot sun. And all the while, he was so aware of her it amazed him that he didn't staple his hand. How could she have gotten under his skin so quickly? He'd only just met her, even though he felt as if he'd known her forever. It had only been that one kiss. That one unbelievable kiss.

He forced himself not to look. To keep his mind and his eyes on the job. It took a great deal of effort, but finally the last shingle was down and the last nail was driven home. He leaned back on his haunches, eyeing the job, making sure nothing had escaped his attention. The chimney needed some work, but that wasn't a priority. If he was planning the job, he'd do that just before he redid the downstairs floor. But he wasn't planning the job. It was time for him to clock out.

"It looks great," Beth said. "You did a wonderful job. I never would have been able to do it this well. And certainly never in one day."

The knife of guilt stabbed him in the solar plexus. He knew she hadn't said that to make him feel like hell, but that's what happened. Damn that Sam Duncan. Why in blazes had he planted this new seed, just when Jarred had managed to kill the roots of the old tree? For God's sake, he'd paid his debt.

Beth cleared her throat and started toward the ladder. "The kids are due home any minute," she said. "I need to start dinner. You'll have to let me know when your flight is so we can get you to the airport on time."

Oh, great. She'd given him a nice thank you and all he'd done was scowl at her. Nice job. Really swift.

She was already at the ladder, not even bothering to wait for him to hold it steady. The thought of her falling set his pulse racing. "Hold on," he said.

She barely looked at him. He clambered over to her, almost losing his own footing to reach her before she'd climbed over the edge of the roof, getting hold of the ladder at the last second. He cursed at himself until she reached the ground, and started all over again when he made his own descent. By the time he'd hit the ground, he was out of oaths and Beth was gone. She must have been in a hurry, trying to get away from him, and he couldn't blame her.

His back hurt. He was so thirsty he could drink a small lake. The sandwich hadn't been near enough for lunch, and his stomach growled its displeasure. So what? Tough beans. He didn't have three kids depending on him. He didn't have a husband who'd left him in the lurch. He didn't have an empty bank account and broken-down old house.

But he sure knew how to bitch about life. If complaining had been an Olympic sport, he'd get the gold without batting an eye.

He shook his head and made his way to the house, the nail gun and the leftover nails in his hands, the weight of his own misery on his back.

Beth was filling a big pot with water as he walked in. She turned her head ever so slightly away from him, which was worse than a slap.

He wanted to say he was sorry. To let her know that none of this was her fault, that he was just a jerk. But he was pretty sure she already knew that.

This was nuts. He put the tools on the counter, then went over to Beth. He put his hands on her shoulders and guided her to a chair. She didn't argue. She just sat down, her gaze flitting everywhere but his face.

He debated sitting across from her, but when he finally captured her big green eyes, he crouched and took both of her hands in his own.

Beth wasn't sure what to do. Part of her wanted to make a mad dash for it, but the other part wanted to understand. Especially when Jarred looked up to meet her gaze. She somehow knew instinctively that he'd crouched down so he wouldn't tower over her. So he wouldn't frighten her. It worked.

"Beth..." he said softly, rubbing the palms of her hands with his thumbs. "Beth, I'm sorry."

"It's okay," she said. "You have nothing to apologize for."

"I do. You know I do. I'm not the brightest of men, but even I recognize that I've been a real jerk. I didn't mean for that to happen."

"Really, it's okay—"

"Wait. Let me get this out, please?"

She nodded, trying to ignore the sensations in her

hands. The rough pads of his thumbs stroking her skin, and the way it gave her goose bumps all over.

"I don't know what Sam told you about me," he began, his voice as gentle with her as it had been when he'd told her daughters his outrageous bedtime story last night. "My parents died in a car accident when I was Caleb's age. I was sent to Lost Springs. I never really fit in there. Sam tried his best, but I never listened to him. I was angry. Angry that I had lost everything. Angry that I was scared every day."

She moved her hands around his until it was she who stroked him. She who squeezed his big hands in comfort, wishing she could do more.

"I was in trouble right away, and I made it a pattern. I ran away, ditched school, stole money. I couldn't break enough rules."

He turned his face away for a moment and she could see the muscles in his neck strain to hold back the emotion she had heard in his voice. "Jarred," she whispered. But he just shook his head to let her know he wasn't ready yet.

Finally, he turned back, his blue eyes surprisingly clear. She wondered why he didn't cry. If he'd ever cried.

"Anyway," he said, "when I was sixteen, I stole Sam's car. It wasn't much, just a beat-up old Chevy with a broken muffler. I made it halfway to Casper before I got stopped by the police. They took me back to Lost Springs. I thought for sure Sam was going to kick me out. But—" He paused again, swallowing hard. "But he didn't. He told the police he'd made a mistake, reporting the car stolen. He said he'd forgotten that he gave me permission to drive it. The cops, they didn't believe him. I mean, it was pretty obvious I'd been trying to fly the coop. But Sam wouldn't budge.''

"Yes, that sounds like Sam," she said. "Always believing the best."

"He was seriously off the mark with me. That night, I took the car again. Only this time, I didn't get caught. I never looked back. And I never saw Sam again until the other day at the auction.''

"I understand now," she said. "Why you came back.''

He nodded. "I owed him. And I wanted him to know I hadn't ended up in jail or on drugs.''

"You wanted him to be proud of you.''

Jarred stood up, his knee popping after being crouched so long. He moved over to the stove, and she noticed that the water was boiling, the steam rising to the vent. He turned off the burner, but he didn't come back to her.

She wanted to go to him. To hold him and soothe his ache. But she didn't have the right. He wasn't hers to comfort.

"I need to stay here," he said, so quietly she had to strain to hear him. "I need to finish this house for you. To see it through. I'm not offering charity, Beth. I'm asking for it.''

Her first instinct was to say yes. But she'd learned a thing or two in the last few years. That her instincts weren't always right. That her children had to come first. That her own emotions could get her into deep trouble.

He finally turned, the pain so clear in his face she wanted to wince. So familiar. And then she understood. She was looking at Caleb as he might look in twenty years or so. Begging for a last shot at redemption.

She stood up, reaching her hand out to him, when the door flew open and Debbi and Karen raced into the kitchen, both of them talking a mile a minute, so loud she could barely make out a word.

"Mom, I rode on a horse!"

"Me, too!"

"I'm gonna tell!"

"You always tell!"

"I do not!"

"You do, too!"

"Hold it!" Beth yelled above the shouting. "Quiet, quiet."

The girls, standing on either side of her, stared daggers at each other while she took a deep, calming breath. She wanted to talk to Jarred, but she couldn't in front of the twins. "Where's Caleb?"

"Outside," Debbi said. "Looking at the roof."

Beth's internal alarm went off, but Jarred had already beaten her to the back door. "I'll go," he said.

She nodded, knowing Jarred would handle the situation, whatever it was, then looked down at the girls. "What I'd like to know is if there's any dirt left in Wyoming, or are you two wearing it all?"

They giggled, the argument forgotten for the moment.

"March right upstairs and get in the tub. I want to see what my children look like again."

They headed out, but Debbi stopped at the door and looked back at her. "I wish you could've seen us."

Beth smiled. "I wish I could have seen you, too."

Then Debbi shot down the hall, her footfalls amazingly loud for such a little girl.

Beth went to the kitchen door to see what was going on with Caleb, but then she saw him with Jarred. The two were talking. Caleb was in his now-familiar stance, hands in pockets, staring hard at the ground, but he was listening. So Beth shut the door and went back to the stove. She turned on the water again, then got the hamburger out of the fridge. As she seasoned the meat, she thought about what Jarred had said. How he needed her. She wanted to help, but was that the wise thing to do?

She didn't want to be dependent on him, or anyone else for that matter. This was her new life, and she owed it to herself and her children to be fully in charge. On the other hand, she was no builder. No carpenter. She barely knew the difference between a wrench and a screwdriver. She ought to jump at the chance to have someone as capable and talented as Jarred take over.

And even if she could put all that aside, she still had to consider the fact that if he stayed, he'd be living here. With her. For quite some time.

The girls already adored him. They'd only grow more enamored as the days went by. Would they be able to let him go?

Caleb might have an even tougher time. He'd deny it to the death, but he liked Jarred. He listened to him. Could she risk having her son come to depend on yet another man who was going to leave?

The water was boiling. She washed her hands, then dropped the pound of spaghetti in. She formed the meat into balls and popped them in the microwave. Once that was done, she got the jar of sauce out of the cupboard and poured it in a pot. Another minute, and she got the cooked meatballs out of the microwave and added them to the sauce. All that was left was the salad.

Her mind kept going over her options. The risks. The gains. Finally, she couldn't put off looking at her own feelings. She was terribly attracted to Jarred. More than any other man she'd ever met. He awakened something inside her, something she hadn't known was there. His touch made her foolish, and his kiss turned her to mush. So what was she going to do with him for two or three months? Would they go the way they were already heading? Would she end up in bed with him?

Part of her hoped so. Which wasn't fair, really. She'd been fine before, never thinking about missing sex. But now that Pandora's box was open, it was going to be a considerable challenge to close it again.

She was just at much at risk as her children of falling in love with Jarred, only to watch him leave. She wasn't at all sure her heart could take it.

The only possible compromise was to let him stay, but keep her distance. If she didn't touch him, or even think of him as anything more than a skilled carpenter, she'd be okay. It wouldn't be easy, but what in her life had been?

She shouldn't let him stay. It was too complicated.

But Sam had asked him to, and she trusted Sam with her life. More important, she trusted Sam with her children's lives. He wouldn't suggest anything that would hurt them, would he?

Sam might have seen them kiss, but he didn't know about the massage. Or the way Jarred made her melt.

But wasn't Sam, in fact, asking her to do a favor

by letting Jarred stay? He'd done so much for her, how could she turn him down?

She groaned, banishing all thoughts of Jarred and Sam as she concentrated on the salad.

It worked. Dinner was almost ready. She went to the door and called out for Jarred and Caleb to come inside. Then she headed to the hallway to get the girls.

"LISTEN, CALEB, it's okay if you don't like horses. I didn't, either. At least not at first."

Caleb looked up at Jarred, his implacable expression not quite as hard to read as he probably hoped. Jarred had too much experience to miss the signs of fear, anger and longing. The boy missed his father. He was frightened of this new place where he had so few friends. And he was mighty furious at the world for changing on him.

"That's all anybody talks about out here," Caleb said. "Stupid horses."

Jarred nodded. "Yeah, Wyoming is like that. But wait till winter. Then all anybody will talk about is snow."

"I hate snow."

"There are some advantages to snow."

"Yeah?"

"Lots of snow days at school. Bet you didn't have those in San Diego."

There it was. The tiniest hint of a grin. Immediately banished of course, but Jarred had seen it. He wished he could do more for the kid. But he had no reason to think he was going to be around to do more. He'd seen Beth's face. Her apprehension and her doubt. He couldn't blame her. Just like Caleb, Beth had no reason to trust him. She'd been chewed up and spit out, and she wasn't likely to be taking any big risks.

He had decided one thing, however. After he got back to Houston, he would call the local construction company and make arrangements for them to finish Beth's house. That was probably the best solution, anyway.

"How come you left here if you like it so much?" Caleb asked.

"I left when I was old enough to keep a job. To take care of myself. I had to find my own way."

"I know where I'm going," Caleb said, his voice sounding much younger as it swelled with his wish. "I'm going back home. I'm going to live with my dad, and I'm going to work with him in his company."

"I'm sure he'll like that," Jarred said. "But first, you need to finish school so you'll be a good partner to him. And before you leave, you have some pretty important business to take care of here."

Caleb didn't acknowledge him in any way. He stared off into the field in back of the house, where the big red barn had once stood.

"I'm gonna speak honestly now, Caleb," Jarred said, putting his hand on the boy's shoulder. "It's not fair, but you've got the hardest job of all out here. Now that I've gotten to know you a little, I can see you're man enough to handle it."

"What do you mean?"

"I mean that someone has to take care of your mother. And your sisters. Someone has to be the man of the house."

"I can't be the man of the house. I'm only nine."

"Nine is plenty old enough to do the job."

"How?"

"By helping your mom. By being nice to her. And helpful. She needs you, son. She needs you more than you can know."

"I'm not your son," he said, jerking his shoulder free.

"That's right. But you're Beth's son."

"It's her fault. We wouldn't have had to leave if she'd—"

"If she'd what?"

"If she'd been a better wife."

Jarred took in a deep breath, then let it out as he moved in front of Caleb. He crouched down, so he was eye to eye with the boy. "Caleb, it's not your mother's fault. I know that's hard to believe, but trust me. You'll understand it someday. You'll see she did the very best that she could for her family. It's up to you to have faith, and to give her the benefit of the doubt."

The boy's lower lip quivered, but he didn't say anything.

"You can do it, Caleb. I know you have it in you."

Just then Jarred heard the back door open. He stood up and turned. Beth called them inside for dinner for the second time.

Caleb started toward the house, and Jarred let him go on ahead, wondering if he'd said anything right. Hoping he hadn't made things worse.

By the time he'd washed and gotten to the table, everyone was seated and Beth was serving the spaghetti and meatballs. She looked at him curiously, and he knew she wanted to know what he'd talked about with Caleb. He'd explain later. On the way to the airport.

"Can we watch *Lion King* after dinner?" Debbi asked.

"No, *101 Dalmatians!*" Karen insisted.

"*Lion King!*"

"*101 Dalmatians!*"

"Quiet!" Beth said. The girls glared at each other, but they obeyed. "Why don't we let our guest choose the video?"

All eyes turned to Jarred. But his gaze went straight to Beth. "I thought—"

"Kids, Jarred is going to be staying with us for a while. Isn't that nice? He's going to help us finish the house."

The girls erupted in wild cheers, bouncing on their chairs like a couple of grasshoppers.

Jarred kept his gaze on their mother. He mouthed, "Are you sure?"

She shook her head and shrugged. But then she gave him a honey of a smile and served him his dinner.

CHAPTER ELEVEN

THE TWINS FINISHED DINNER first. Of course, half the spaghetti sauce was on their faces instead of in their stomachs, but Beth didn't mind. They were so thrilled about Jarred staying that their manners were subverted by their enthusiasm. Strangely enough, Beth found herself a bit exhilarated. Now that she'd committed to the plan, she allowed herself the luxury of thinking things would turn out great. Her house would become a home and a means of keeping the family fed. When they were finished, the whole second floor would consist of guest rooms. She would stay downstairs in what was now Caleb's room, and the kids would all be in the attic. With the wall knocked down in the living room, she could create a warm and cozy parlor, enhanced by the fireplace and her grandfather's antiques.

It could work. It really could. She was a good cook, although she wanted to expand her repertoire, and she could certainly be a good hostess. It wouldn't be easy on the kids—they'd have to learn to be quiet in the house when guests were there, but she chose to believe in them.

It had to work.

"Do you want to talk about the plans tonight?" Jarred asked.

She should. There wasn't time to waste, but she

just couldn't. Not tonight. "Why don't we do that first thing in the morning?" she suggested. "I think tonight we should all go to town and get some ice cream. That is, if you guys want to."

The twins yelled a resounding "Yeah!" and even Caleb managed to give her a little smile.

She pointed at the girls. "You. Upstairs. I want those faces shiny clean."

They didn't waste a moment, shooting out of their chairs and barreling out of the kitchen.

"And change your shirts!" Beth called after them. She turned back to Caleb and Jarred. They'd both cleaned their plates, having had two helpings each. Caleb surprised her by remaining at the table. Lately, he couldn't seem to wait to get away from her. But he sat there now, shooting secret glances at Jarred every few minutes.

"This was great," Jarred said. "Best spaghetti I've had in years."

"It's an old family recipe. Not *my* family. But it's good."

He smiled. "I'd like to hear about your family," he said.

The chair scraped as Caleb bolted up. He left the room at a half walk, half run. Beth felt herself deflate like a balloon. He was so sensitive. It was like being in a minefield.

"I'm sorry," Jarred said. "I should have realized…"

"It's not your fault. He's just—"

"Scared."

"Yes. And I don't blame him."

"Give him time, Beth. He'll come around."

"I hope so." She stood up and started to stack the

dinner dishes. "I think a good dose of Rocky Road will help. At least for tonight."

"You're right. Nothing calms me down better than a double scoop." He stood, too, and brought the glasses to the sink. Beth put the dishes down and turned on the water. "Don't you have a phone call to make?"

He nodded. "I'll help first."

She shook her head. "Nope. I'm fine. But I appreciate the offer. You go on ahead."

He didn't exactly listen to her. Instead, he went back to the table, picked up the last of the silverware and the empty pasta bowl. After he put those on the counter, he smiled, and for a moment, she thought he was going to say something. He didn't. He just went over to the phone on the other side of the room.

She tried not to listen, and succeeded when the water was running. But once it was quiet, she couldn't help but hear him talk to his assistant. Jarred asked her to send his clothes and his mail. Beth gave him the address, and after Jarred repeated it, he went on to discuss his company.

He talked for a long while, and Beth realized just how much he was leaving behind to help with her house. It wasn't fair. She had no business taking him away like this. Guilt, as familiar to her as breathing, urged her to tell him that she'd made a mistake. That she didn't need him. But that wasn't true. Despite all her misgivings, she had to admit she did need his help. On her own, it would take at least a year to get the house in shape. Probably a lot longer. And she'd never do the job as well as Jarred.

So instead of letting the guilt win, she turned the

water on again. To make it even harder to hear, she hummed an old Beatles song.

He got off the phone just as she put the last pot in the drainer.

"All set?" she asked.

He nodded. "I'll have my things by day after tomorrow, latest."

She reached for the dish towel, but he got to it first. "My turn to dry."

"You don't have to. You're already doing too much."

"Okay," he said, putting down the towel. "Here's the deal." He took her by the shoulders and turned her so they faced each other. "Say thank-you."

"Excuse me?"

"I said, say thank-you."

"Thank you."

"You're welcome," he said back. "Now we're finished with the gratitude portion. You can't say it again until the house is finished. Then you're allowed to say it once more."

"Oh, really?"

He nodded, looking very serious, except for the mischief in his eyes.

"What if I break this deal?"

"Punishment will be swift and severe."

"Oh, my."

"You got that right. It won't be pretty."

She knew he was kidding, but she still felt her tummy go all squishy and her cheeks heat up. He hadn't said a suggestive word, yet all she could think of was naughty ways he could carry out her sentence. She stepped back, dislodging his hands from her shoulders. "All right," she said, turning away. She was sure he knew exactly where her thoughts had gone.

His low chuckle confirmed her worst fears. "On second thought," he said, "say thank-you again. Please."

She nudged him with her shoulder, causing him to take a step to his right.

"Hey!"

"You're not the only one to enact swift punishment," she said, trying to hide her blush by focusing on the sink.

"So you want to play that game, eh?" he teased, moving in behind her and placing his outstretched arms on either side of her. He was so close she could feel his heat all the way down her back. Although he didn't touch her, she knew if she took even the slightest step, she'd bump into him. The urge to do just that was great, made greater by the memory of the kiss on the rooftop.

"Hmm," he said, his voice low and gravelly, very close to her ear. "The question is, what punishment suits the crime?"

Acting as if he wasn't turning her knees to Jell-O or making her heart pound in her chest, she casually turned on the water, using the pull-out nozzle to clean the sink.

"I'm not the one breaking the rules," she said.

"Rules? What rules?"

"The rules we both know shouldn't be broken."

"I don't know what you're talking about," he said, so near now that his breath heated the back of her neck.

Beth closed her eyes and drew on every ounce of

strength she had. "The rules," she whispered, "about you staying here. About not doing anything foolish."

"Foolish?" he asked, finally touching the edge of her ear with his lips. "Nothing I could do to you would be foolish."

She shivered all the way down to her toes. All she had to do was turn. That's what he was waiting for. And she could be in his arms, drowning in his kiss, melting like hot wax until she was nothing more than a puddle on the floor. But if she did... Now that he'd decided to stay, the game had changed. The outcome held too great a risk. She might have talked herself into a one-night stand with a handsome stranger, but an affair? Never. She wasn't the type.

Then she felt him nip her earlobe with his teeth, very gently...a move designed to make her lose her mind. Seconds before she lost her senses completely, she raised the nozzle, fast, over her shoulder.

"Hey! Cut it out!"

She turned then, focusing the jet of water on his face. He sputtered and used his hands as a shield, but it was no use. She might not know how to shingle a roof, but she was an expert at washing up.

She heard Debbi and Karen run into the room, and Jarred's pleas for mercy were drowned out by her daughters' screaming laughter.

Beth turned off the water. Jarred stared at her as if she'd gone nuts on him, which, in a way, she had. She'd soaked his hair, his face dripped and his shirt looked as if she'd just pulled it out of the wash.

She had no business laughing, but he looked so...so...adorable.

"You think this is funny?" he asked, wiping his eyes.

"Oh, yes," she said. "I just wish I had a camera."

He grabbed the dish towel off the counter and rubbed his face with it. When he brought the towel down, he looked at her through narrowed eyes. "You realize, of course, what you've done."

"Yeah," she said. "Cooled your jets."

He shook his head slowly. "You've thrown down the gauntlet. From now on, all bets are off. It's war."

"War?"

He nodded. "When you least expect it, when your guard is down—that's when I'll strike. I will get you back."

"Ha," she said, forcing herself to stop grinning. "I'd like to see you try."

He raised one damp eyebrow. "You will, little lady. You will."

"Are we still going out for ice cream?" Debbi asked.

Beth turned, just now noticing what the twins had on. They were dressed in their daily uniform of shorts and T-shirts, but each girl had a towel wrapped around her neck, hanging down behind them like capes. "What's this?"

The twins looked at each other, then turned to the dripping Jarred. They each raised one hand, which was balled into a tight fist. After shaking their fist three times in a row, they slapped them across their hearts.

Jarred stared at them, probably wondering if the whole family was certifiable, but then he repeated their gesture exactly. Three shakes, then a slap to the chest.

Her gaze went back to the girls. Their reaction completely startled her. Their eyes widened, their little mouths dropped open, and she could practically see the visible waves of their puppy-love crush waft across the kitchen, aimed directly at Jarred.

"What's that about?" she asked.

"I have no idea," Jarred said. "But then, this family is full of surprises, isn't it?"

She nodded. "Don't you think you'd better get out of those wet clothes? I mean, we want to get ice cream before midnight."

He scowled at her and shook his head in a dire warning. Then he left the room.

Beth leaned against the kitchen sink, sighing in relief. She'd escaped, but barely. One more second, and her daughters would have walked in on a PG-13 scene starring Mom and the houseguest. Not good.

Now, if she could only stop herself from the awful feeling it would have been worth it.

SOMEHOW, JARRED HAD managed to make up yet another bedtime story for the twins. It was mostly a retelling of an old Fractured Fairytale he'd seen on Rocky and Bullwinkle, but it starred Galaxy Man. The girls were finally asleep, and Jarred was ready for bed, too. He stood up, pressing his hand to the small of his back where the pain had settled into a dull roar. The last time he'd fixed a roof, he'd been a lot younger and more accustomed to the particular movements the job required.

He rubbed his back for a moment, then caught a glimpse of the stack of Galaxy Man comic books on the makeshift desk sitting in the corner. What was it about the superhero the girls liked so much? Weren't they supposed to like Caspar or Little Lulu? Barbie? Ponies?

He picked up the latest volume, checking out the drawing on the cover. Galaxy Man stood ready to fight evil, his fist over his heart, his cape flowing in a two-dimensional wind. Something about him struck a chord, but Jarred couldn't figure out what. Although he had seen the character before, he'd never really paid attention. Now, though, the feeling that he knew someone who looked like the cartoon hero teased him. He shrugged, putting the comic back on the stack. It wasn't important.

He turned to leave, but stopped when he saw Beth standing at the door. She was already in her night-gown and pale blue chenille robe. She'd pushed her short blond hair back with a thin band, and he drank in the sight of her clean, beautiful face. In some ways, she looked as young as the twins, mostly around the eyes. Bright, big, friendly eyes, filled with curiosity and a trust that was odd in this day and age. No wonder he wanted her. She was a fountain of youth, a tonic to his aching muscles and his tired soul.

"I owe you something," she whispered.

"What?"

She held up the tube of vanilla ointment. "I know your back has been hurting."

"It's okay. Nothing a shower won't fix."

Her gaze went to the floor as she took a step back. Jarred hadn't meant to do that. He walked across the bedroom, then led Beth into the hallway, closing the door behind him. "I didn't mean I didn't want you to—"

"It's okay," she said, holding the tube out for him. "I'm pretty tired. I'll just—"

"No," he interrupted. "I'd like it if you—"

"You should shower and—"

"I will," he said. "I will. But it won't take long. And then, if you wouldn't mind?"

She met his gaze again. "I'll wait."

He smiled. "Good."

"But, Jarred?"

"Yes?"

"It's only a back rub. For medicinal purposes."

He nodded. "Well, sure. That's all I expected."

"I'm not kidding."

He took her free hand and headed farther away from the girls' bedroom. "About those rules," he said, stopping at the attic stairs.

"I wasn't kidding about that, either."

He faced her again. "I know. I'm going to be here for a while, and we shouldn't…"

"No, we shouldn't."

"It would be confusing for the kids," he said.

"And you'll be leaving."

He nodded, focusing on her mouth. The perfect shade of pink, and it didn't come from any lipstick. Her white teeth were so small, just like her. But her responsibilities were so big…too big. Thank goodness Sam had talked him into staying.

"Jarred?"

He blinked, coming back to the conversation. "Well, I'll just go up now…"

"I'll wait for a while…"

"Ten minutes?"

She nodded.

"Okay, then."

She stilled her hand but she didn't let him go. Not that she was touching him. But the way she looked at him held him steadier than any touch could have.

"Maybe…" he whispered.

Her mouth opened a little. Her perfect pink mouth.

He leaned forward slowly, as if pulled by an invisible wire. Even if he'd wanted to stop, he didn't think it was possible.

She kept her eyes open until the very last second. Until he touched her lips with his. Then her lids fluttered closed, and his followed suit.

He took it slow and easy. Tasting her with a flick of his tongue, breathing in her scent. Then he wanted more, and he stepped closer to her, wrapping her petite body in his arms. He felt her own exploration. Her hands wrapping around his neck, her exquisite teeth nibbling on his lower lip.

He sighed as he felt himself relax. No pain, no soreness. Only Beth in his arms. Her taste and her scent and her feel erased the rest of the universe. There was only the two of them.

Kissing her harder, he dipped between her teeth, shivering at the moist heat inside her. She opened her mouth wider, and then he couldn't think anymore. All he could do was kiss her and be kissed back, run his hands down her slender body and feel her fingers in his hair.

He heard her moan, or maybe it was his moan. Then he heard a soft clunk as she let go of the tube and it hit the floor.

She stiffened in his arms. Her hands went to his shoulders, and her lips moved away, breaking the spell with a finality that made him groan.

She stepped back, shaking her head. Her fingers went to her lips as if she couldn't believe what she'd done. Her gaze turned troubled, confused.

"Beth," he whispered.

She shook her head. "I can't."

"Yes, you can. You can."

"No. It's not going to be like this. It can't be like this."

"But—"

"Jarred," she said, her back straightening as her hand slid down from her lips. "I can't do this. I won't. And if you can't..." She looked away for the briefest of seconds, and when her gaze came back to him, it was filled with determination. "If you can't, then I'll have to ask you to leave."

He didn't move for a long while. He thought about what she'd said. About what it meant.

He'd see her every day. Every night.

They'd touch in the hallway, or at the kitchen sink.

He'd hear her in the shower.

He'd smell lilacs when she walked by.

Could he do it? Was it possible for him to want her like this and not touch her again? Especially when he knew she wanted it, too? Of that, he was certain. She'd kissed him with want, with a hunger she couldn't hide. The ultimatum wasn't about wanting, though. It was about thinking. Being smart. Not going somewhere that could only end one way—badly. She was asking him to respect her, and her family, and her decision.

Was he man enough to do that? To obey his mind instead of his body? The truth was, he didn't know. But he was going to find out.

"I'll stay," he said. "And I won't touch you again."

She swallowed. Nodded.

"But I need you to know that it won't be easy. I want you, Beth. I want you so much it..." He stopped, took a breath. "I give you my word I won't touch you again."

"Thank you," she whispered.

"Beth?"

She nodded.

"My door will be open. Remember that. It will always be open."

CHAPTER TWELVE

BETH WAS ALREADY AWAKE and in the kitchen fixing breakfast when she got the phone call from Mrs. King asking if she wanted to temp at the dentist's office. The job would last three days while Phyllis Long, the regular receptionist, went to take care of her ailing mother in Denver.

Beth's first reaction was to say no. She didn't want to leave Jarred to work alone. But then in the next breath, she changed her mind. Jarred wouldn't miss her help for a few days. And the time apart would be good for both of them.

She'd had a bad night. Fitful and anxious, she'd gotten up four times and had trouble getting back to sleep each time. Working at an unfamiliar office would keep her alert, and even more important, it would keep her mind occupied.

She told Mrs. King, the office manager, that she'd be there at nine, then she hurried to get breakfast on the table so she could go get dressed in something nicer than the jeans and T-shirt she'd selected this morning.

The oatmeal was bubbling in the pot, and the coffee had just finished dripping into the carafe when she heard a footfall behind her.

Expecting Caleb or the girls, she turned to find Jarred standing in the doorway. He was in the same jeans and polo shirt he'd worn that first day, and his hair was still damp, combed back so she could see that he hadn't had a good night's rest, either. His eyes looked tired, and the lines that bracketed his mouth seemed deeper.

"I was going to do that," he said, nodding at the pot on the stove.

"It's okay. I was up. Coffee's ready."

He walked over to the cupboard where she kept the mugs and brought out two. Then he went to the coffeepot and poured her a cup first. He handed it to her silently, holding the hot sides so she could take the handle and not burn herself. The small gesture made her chest tighten. Here was a man who was orphaned at nine, who ran away from home at sixteen to live on his own, and who had the best manners of anyone she knew. Compared to Jarred, her husband seemed to have been raised by wolves.

"I heard the phone," he said. "Is everything okay?"

She went back to stirring the oatmeal as he leaned against the counter, drinking his coffee. "Yes, fine. Actually, it was a job. For me."

"Oh?"

"I do temporary work. I think I might have mentioned that before. Anyway, they need me at the dentist's office for a few days. I figured you'd be okay if I wasn't here. I hope that's true."

He nodded. "I'll be fine. What about the kids?"

"They'll go to Mrs. Oliver's again after school. Her kids like mine, and they have horses, so everyone's happy when they get together."

"That's lucky."

"Yes," she agreed. "Yes, it is."

He sipped his coffee again, and Beth wished the awkwardness that hung between them would go away. She wished they'd never kissed. And that she hadn't lain awake all night thinking about his lips on hers.

"I'll go up and look at the plans right after breakfast," Jarred said. "I think that the next order of business is fixing the inside walls."

"Sounds good," she agreed, although what she wanted to tell him was far more personal. She wanted to tell him she liked him. That she liked the easy way they talked. The sound of his laughter. The way his hair looked when he was fresh from his shower. And that she didn't like the fact that she felt as if she had to walk on eggshells now.

"Beth, about last night..."

She took the pot of oatmeal from the burner and put it on a hot pad on the counter. She busied herself getting bowls, not trusting herself to look at him.

"I intend to keep my promise," he said. "You don't have to worry."

"I'm not worried. I have no doubts that you'll be a perfect gentleman. You've been nothing if not courteous since you got here."

"Courteous? Me?" He chuckled in that low way of his.

"Why does that make you laugh?" she asked, finally turning toward him again. His smile looked more melancholy than amused.

"I've never been accused of being courteous before, that's all. A few other choice things, but never courteous."

"But you are. You're very gallant."

He shook his head. "Come on. I'm not even close."

She folded her arms across her chest. "I think the girls are right about you."

"Oh?"

"They think you're wonderful. Or hadn't you noticed?"

He pushed off from the counter, heading toward the other side of the room. "They're kids. They don't know better."

"I'm not a kid."

He looked back at her, over his shoulder. "I'm not wonderful, Beth."

She stopped, the teasing comment she was about to make stilled on her tongue. His message was clear: he'd respect her wishes, but it wouldn't stop him from wanting more. Wanting something quite ungentlemanly.

Her body responded to his message more quickly than her wits. Before she lost control and said something she'd regret, she walked across the kitchen and into the hallway. Straight to Caleb's room. But before she knocked, she leaned her forehead on the cool wood door.

What had the man done to her? It wasn't as if she hadn't been around attractive men before. But no one had ever affected her like this. She felt as though she'd swallowed a potion, an aphrodisiac that worked only when Jarred was close by. It wasn't smart. It wasn't funny. And she didn't have a clue what to do about it.

She stood straight again, putting her dilemma on hold, and knocked on Caleb's door. "Breakfast," she called. Then she knocked once more, waiting until she heard his mumbled reply.

She headed toward the stairs to wake up the girls, but they were already up. She heard laughter from above, the sound making her smile. Was any sound quite as wonderful as a child's laughter? Beth thanked God that the twins had such good temperaments. They'd probably go nuts at puberty, what with needing to establish their own identities, but until then, they were a pleasure, plain and simple.

It was getting late, and she still had to get ready for work, so she rushed up the stairs, calling out for the girls to hurry up and have breakfast, but she didn't wait for their reply. She had her shirt half off by the time she swung her bedroom door shut behind her.

JARRED SERVED THE KIDS, then helped himself to a bowl of oatmeal. He normally didn't eat the stuff, especially not with all the brown sugar and milk the twins slathered on it, but when he tasted the cereal, it wasn't half bad.

Caleb liked his plain, it seemed. He ate steadily, not looking at anything in particular. Just lost in his unhappy world.

Then Jarred looked at the twins, each of them playing with their food, making designs in the oatmeal with their spoons. It occurred to him that it must be nice, having a twin.

Jarred took a sip of his coffee, wondering what it was that had him feeling so peculiar. Beth? No, not at the moment, although she made him feel plenty peculiar. Then he got it. It wasn't one thing—it was all of it. The children at the breakfast table. The gallon of milk. The Daffy Duck glasses. He felt as if he were in a play about a family, but he didn't understand his part.

This was something new. Even though he'd been at the orphanage for a great deal of his childhood, he'd never once felt the security that these kids wore like old shoes. He'd never experienced the quiet calm that came from knowing the same people would be there the next day and the day after that.

Even with the divorce, and with Caleb's hard time adjusting, there was peace in this house. Mostly because all of them had a stake in one another. They cared what happened, and it mattered if someone was hurt or happy. This place, these people, they played for keeps.

He'd dreamed about a family like this for years. Like something out of a television show, only better because it wasn't perfect. You could mess up with a family like this, and it wouldn't be so bad. They'd take you back, no matter what.

It occurred to him that he hadn't had this even when his parents had been alive. He didn't remember all that much about them, except that they were always going somewhere. To him, the world had consisted of motel rooms and diners. Of passing trains and buildings flying by the window of an old car.

Transient. Slippery. It had all been awash in a tension he'd thought was normal. It wasn't until years later, after he was in his twenties, that he realized other people didn't live in a constant state of dread.

"Jarred?"

He looked over at Debbi. She had done something to her hair. Put in a whole mess of clips with little bugs and bows on them. He checked, and Karen had similar adornments. "Yeah?"

"Can we stay here today? And help you?"

"I don't think so, kiddo. I think your mother wants you to go to school."

"Can't you talk to her? I bet if you ask her, she'll let us stay."

"No, she won't," a feminine voice stated calmly.

They all turned to see Beth standing at the entry. She'd changed into a real nice beige skirt and blouse. Her hair looked soft and pretty, and she'd put on makeup, too. Nothing major. Just enough to make her eyes and her lips even more beautiful.

"You're going to see Melissa and Tony after school. And the bus will be here in about three hot minutes, so finish up and then wash your faces."

"Do we have to?"

Beth walked into the kitchen, working on the cuff button of her blouse, which didn't seem to be cooperating. She struggled for another minute, and then she walked over to where Jarred was sitting and stuck her arm out in front of her. "Would you?"

He nodded, wiping his hands on his jeans before he touched her. It only took him a few seconds to help her. As soon as it was done, she withdrew her arm and walked over to get some hot coffee.

She started talking to the kids, but he didn't listen. He was too busy thinking about the moment before. The casual way she'd given him her arm.

He'd undressed and dressed plenty of women in his life. He was better at unhooking bra straps than he was at doing his own neckties. But what he'd done for Beth wasn't like that. He'd just been helping her out.

It was as if he was part of this family. Someone she could take for granted.

For the second time that morning, he got it. This revelation was stronger, though. Strong enough to make his head spin. He wanted to be taken for granted. He wanted to be part of the flow of a family. He wanted to be counted on. "Well, I'll be damned," he whispered.

"Pardon?" Beth asked.

"Nothing," he said. But it wasn't nothing. It was a detour in a road he'd long believed would run straight and true till the end of his days.

BETH KNEW SOMETHING was off even before she and the kids saw the house. She couldn't pin it down, and for the last half mile, she'd been convinced that it was just the expectation that Jarred was waiting for her. That she'd be with him for the whole evening.

But then, as they drew closer to the old house and she saw the front lawn, she understood her premonition.

Jarred had been very busy. There were building tools, equipment and lumber—a veritable hardware store in front of her porch. "Oh, my heavens," she whispered as she slowed the car to a stop.

The girls were out in a flash, hopping up and down, hugging each other, then running to look at the goodies Jarred had bought.

"He did it!" Karen shouted.

"I knew he would!" Debbi answered.

"Galaxy Man!"

Beth shook her head at the girls as she stepped out of the car. She didn't understand that last bit, but she had bigger things to think about at the moment. It must have cost Jarred a fortune. How on earth was she going to pay him back?

"Is this our stuff, Mom?"

She turned to Caleb, standing a few feet in back of her. "I think so," she said.

"Dad sent it," he said quietly. Hopefully.

"I don't think so, honey." She wished that it had been Caleb's father who had made such a generous move. "I think this is from Jarred."

Caleb didn't acknowledge her. He just headed inside, moving quickly through the well-organized rows of building materials. Not looking down. Not looking back. Watching him twisted the knife that was always in her heart now.

"Mommy, look!"

She shifted her gaze from the closed front door to Karen. Her little girl was holding a level that was almost as big as she was.

"That's great, honey," Beth said. She started toward the front door, amazed at how much Jarred had bought in only one day. She also had a good idea what it had cost, since she'd done the budget on the materials she'd need. Except, from what she could see, Jarred had gotten top-quality everything, instead of cutting corners the way she'd planned to.

She was looking at thousands of dollars. Dollars she didn't have.

On the other hand, she couldn't help but feel a sense of excitement. It was as if she were seeing her dreams come to life. The future she wanted for her children made material, right here in the boxes of nails and tiles and two-by-fours. She'd figure out a way to pay him back. But in the meantime, he'd make her family secure.

The front door opened and Jarred came outside. Caleb was with him, although from where she stood it didn't seem voluntary. Jarred had his arm firmly around Caleb's shoulder while her son tried to squirm away.

"Let me go," Caleb said. "I don't want to."

"Sure you do, scout," Jarred said brightly.

"Sure he does what?" Beth asked, hating that her attention was immediately drawn to Jarred's height and strength. That she knew the form of his muscles beneath his shirt, and that the image filled her with longing.

"I've offered Caleb a job," Jarred said. "As my assistant."

"I don't have to," Caleb said. "You're not my father."

"Of course I'm not your father. But Beth is your mother, and she needs help."

"I help her."

Jarred turned so he faced Caleb, and still holding on to him lest he bolt away, the big man crouched so he was eye level with the boy. "I know you do, son. You help her a lot. This is another opportunity. And I'll pay you."

"Pay me?" Caleb stopped squirming.

Jarred nodded. "Five dollars an hour."

"Hold it," Beth said, approaching the guys. "He doesn't need to get paid to help. It's part of his responsibility as a member of this household. Besides, he already gets an allowance, don't you, Caleb."

He looked at her, burning her with the passion and anger in his young gaze. "I can still get paid," he said. "You can't stop me if he wants to pay me."

"I can't?"

Caleb looked at Jarred, jerking his shoulders free. "I'll do it. I'll work so hard. And I'll save the money and I'll get on the bus and I'll go live with Dad." He turned on Beth. "You can't stop me if I can pay for it with my own money."

"Caleb, honey—"

The boy ran past her, straight into the house, and slammed the door behind him. Beth felt her insides deflate. All the joy and anticipation she'd felt only a moment ago vanished like smoke in the wind. All Caleb wanted was for his father to rescue him. She didn't have the heart to tell her son that it was a wish that wouldn't come true. Dan didn't want Caleb to live with him. He'd made that very clear. But how could she ever say that to her baby?

"I messed up, didn't I?" Jarred said. He'd stood and moved closer to her. Close enough for him to reach out and touch her arm lightly.

She shook her head. "It's not your fault. It's much more than the money."

"His father," Jarred said softly, so the twins wouldn't hear.

Beth nodded, fighting tears. "It's…complicated."

"I know."

Beth tried a smile, but it didn't take. "So what's all this?" she asked, looking at the hardware.

"Just part of the deal," he said.

"What deal?"

"The deal I made with Sam."

"I don't see Sam around," she said. "But what I do see is an awful lot of expensive equipment."

"Hey, I own a construction company. I get it all at cost."

"Even at cost—"

"Beth," he said, changing his feather-light touch

to a firm grip just above her elbow. "It's all right. I wouldn't have done this if I didn't want to."

"I'll pay you back," she vowed. "Every dime."

"No," he said. "You don't owe me anything."

"Dammit, Jarred, this is my home and my rules. I've already gone overboard by letting you do so much work, but I won't be beholden for all of this."

"Beholden? You won't be. At least not to me. You might have to tell Sam thank-you. He's the one I bought this for. Not you. He's the one I'm paying back."

"That's all semantics," she said.

"No, it's a debt. One I've needed to pay back for a long time."

"Then why aren't you building a new wing at the ranch?"

"Because I'm needed here," he said. "Because I would want to be here even if Sam hadn't asked me."

Beth started to protest, but stopped when she met his steady gaze. His light-blue eyes, always so startling against his tan skin and dark hair, made her argument disappear. He was telling her the truth. He needed her just as badly as she needed him.

And she saw something else. He wanted her as much as she wanted him.

Something was going on here that she barely understood. It had more to do with broken hearts than lust, although lust was undeniably there. This was about his past and her future. Her dreams and his regrets.

Somehow, it was bigger than the both of them.

She nodded her agreement.

CHAPTER THIRTEEN

THEIR DAYS BEGAN to take on a routine that was at once comforting and unsettling for a man who'd been on his own his whole life. Jarred was almost always the first one up, so he took care of breakfast. Beth offered to cook dinner, but Jarred took them out while she was working. Sam had dropped by again, and Jarred had taken the opportunity to speak to him about Caleb. About how to help. But all Sam had said was to trust his instincts. To listen. To remember. So far, nothing had changed at all, even though Jarred was trusting and listening to beat the band.

It was hard for him to believe that it was already Friday. He'd called his office every day, only to find out that things were well under control and that he needn't worry. It was stupid, but it bothered him that he was so dispensable. From the tone of his assistant's voice, it sounded as if his company ran better when he wasn't around. Great.

But that was a small price to pay for the satisfaction he felt at the work he did here. The house was starting to take shape. It had a long way to go, yes, but he could already see it finished in his head. It would be a comfortable safe haven, especially in winter. A solid home for Beth and her children, and a treat for any visitor lucky enough to stay.

He'd already decided he'd come back. Maybe next

summer. Just to make sure everything held up, and
that Beth was okay. By then, she'd know what
worked and what needed changing in the house, and
it would make a good vacation for him to putter
around.

The kids would be older. By then, he hoped that
Caleb would have settled down and accepted the sep-
aration from his father. With school and friends,
Jarred felt sure the boy would be all right, but he had
to admit, he worried about Caleb now.

He'd turned into a good helper, working every
night after school. He was taciturn, sure, but Jarred
didn't fault him for that. The kid did what he was
told, and he did it as well as he could. There were
many men Jarred had worked with who didn't have
those qualities.

It wasn't Caleb's work habits that concerned
Jarred, it was his goal. Caleb was determined to go
live with his dad. When Beth wasn't around, the boy
talked about his father incessantly. About the time he
took Caleb to Disneyland, and how he'd promised to
take him to a baseball game. Jarred let him talk. But
at least once during every conversation, he'd remind
Caleb about the adventures that awaited him here in
Wyoming. He'd touch on the fact that people change,
and that sometimes a man can't always get what he
wants. It wasn't any use, however. Caleb didn't seem
to hear him. Or care.

It wasn't hard to see why Sam had asked him to
stay. The old man had seen how much Caleb was like
Jarred at the same age, and he figured Jarred would
be able to help. But, once more, Jarred was afraid he
was going to disappoint Sam. Despite following his
old friend's advice, he didn't think he was helping at

all. Caleb was locked up tight, and Jarred simply didn't have the key.

He put his coffee cup in the sink and stretched. He felt looser, but not much. He'd tried to put the ointment on his own back, which was more a trick for a contortionist than a construction worker, but at least he'd reached his shoulders. Hot baths had also helped. He'd kill for a good rubdown, especially by Oscar, the old Polish masseur at his gym in Houston.

He glanced at the clock and headed toward the bathroom, where he'd been working on the bathtub tiles. He wouldn't finish the job today, not when Beth was due home in a little over an hour. Tomorrow, he'd put in the grout. Then he had to replace the toilet, the pedestal sink and the molding around the mirror.

He'd already planned dinner. It was Friday night, and Beth's job had stretched out an extra day. She had to be beat. He'd called a local caterer, and she'd agreed to fix them a turkey dinner with all the trimmings and deliver it to the house. No fuss, no muss. And turkey sandwiches for lunch tomorrow.

Beth would be pleased. He knew she would. She'd get that smile on her face, the one with all the bewilderment in it. The one that made him feel like some kind of hero just because he gave her coffee, or remembered she didn't like orange juice. The smile that had become a daily goal of his.

Friday night. Back home, he'd almost always eaten at the restaurant three blocks from his apartment. Inevitably, he'd order the steak, or the fish, depending on what Christy, the waitress, recommended. He'd finish dinner with a slice of pie sometimes. Mostly, though, he didn't have dessert. Then he'd walk home, turn on ESPN and veg out. Nine times out of ten, he'd wake up in the morning, sitting in his big leather chair, the TV still on.

Some life, eh? A hell of a lot quieter than this place, that's for sure. No kids charging down the stairs, no twins in their cotton towel capes running over the furniture. No arguments about who got the bathroom and whose turn it was to put the dishes away.

A guy would have to be nuts to trade in the peace and quiet for all this ruckus. And Jarred wasn't nuts.

But it was kind of weird.... He didn't miss ESPN at all. And he didn't miss those dinners at the Mason Jar. And he sure as hell didn't miss falling asleep out of sheer boredom.

BETH OPENED THE DOOR to a scent so heavenly, she thought for a moment that she'd come to the wrong house. Instead of the metallic odor of paint, or the dusty chalk of plaster, her kitchen smelled like Thanksgiving.

The closer she moved to the table, the farther her jaw dropped open. A gorgeous turkey, at least twenty-five pounds, sat in the center, its brown and crispy skin unable to contain the juices that oozed down the sides. It rested on a silver platter, garnished with roasted vegetables and parsley. Then there was a big steaming casserole of stuffing, laden with corn and mushrooms and walnuts. Another bowl held broccoli, the one vegetable the whole family liked. Even the little touches were there, like the gravy, rolls and cranberry sauce.

It was unbelievable! Five places had been set, and

Jarred had put a couple of wineglasses by both of their plates.

"Surprise."

She whirled around at the sound of his voice to find him leaning casually against the kitchen doorway. He was wearing a navy chambray shirt tucked into a well-worn pair of button-fly blue jeans. Freshly showered, his cheeks smooth from a recent shave, his hair combed back, still damp, he was the best-looking thing she'd ever seen. "You cooked this?"

He shook his head. "Nope. But I found someone who would. I figured you wouldn't want to be stuck behind a stove tonight. Not after the long week you've had."

"I'm...speechless. It's wonderful. Where did you get it?"

"The local caterer," he said, pushing off from the door to walk slowly toward her. "Where are the kids?"

"Oh, heavens," she said. "That was my surprise. They're having dinner at Mrs. Oliver's house tonight. I figured you deserved a peaceful evening."

He smiled. "And did you get me a watch fob, too?"

She got his reference to the O. Henry story immediately. "Yes, I did. So where are my hair combs?"

He'd moved next to her. Close. She could feel him, somehow, even though no part of their bodies touched. "Thank you," she said, but she wasn't sure if it was for the dinner surprise or the fact that he was here, waiting for her.

He nodded. Slowly. Twice.

She realized that he'd hypnotized her with that nod.

There was no choice but to meet his gaze, to feel his heat. She had to lean forward. She had to feel his lips on hers once more; it wasn't a choice. But then he moved, breaking the spell, making her flush with her wanton thoughts.

He coughed and walked quickly to the counter where a bottle of zinfandel sat uncorked. Without turning, he said, "Can I pour you a glass?"

"Please," she said.

He seemed startled to realize he didn't have glasses in front of him. She grabbed the two from the table and brought them to the counter.

"How did it go today?" She was finally growing accustomed to asking this at the end of each day, and hearing him talk about her own house in response.

"Good. I got a lot of the bathroom done. We'll all have to use the upstairs one for a few days."

"Okay. Just remind me to tell everyone when they get back."

He handed her a half-filled glass and took the other for himself. "When, exactly, will that be?"

"Around nine. I don't even have to pick them up. Dorothy is going to drop them off."

"Nice," he said, then nodded at the table. "We should eat before it all gets cold."

"Should we? We could wrap it up and have it for dinner tomorrow night."

"But then what would we have for dinner?"

"We could always call for a pizza," she suggested, with as little enthusiasm as she felt.

He shook his head. "Nope. The kids can eat leftovers. Tonight, we're going to eat well, and we're going to eat quietly, and there isn't going to be even one discussion about Galaxy Man, the Little Mermaid or any other fictional character.''

She held her fingers up to her mouth in shock. "I... I don't know if I can," she said. "I don't remember how."

He walked over to her seat and pulled the chair out. "I'll help you," he said.

She sat down, allowing him the privilege of scooting her in properly. Then he took her napkin, which was linen, not paper—and not hers—and opened it with a flourish, placing the burgundy rectangle neatly on her lap.

She was glad that she hadn't had time to change. Still in her work clothes, she felt more like a lady and less like a mommy than she had in years.

Jarred went to the turkey and held up the carving knife and long-pronged fork. "Dark? White?"

"White, please."

He concentrated hard on making a perfect job of the bird, while she concentrated on him. On the problem that had started the first day he'd arrived, and had gotten worse each day since. It kept her up late at night as she lay in her empty bed. It woke her early as she listened for his footfalls on the staircase in the morning. The problem was that she liked having him here. Way too much. Way, way too much.

It startled her, the speed with which she'd grown to count on him. How they'd created a smooth routine that sped them through their busy days with a minimum of fuss. She knew she could count on him to help out with the kids if she ran late. He made it easy for her to accept his largesse and expertise.

But mostly, she just felt good when she was with him. A good she'd never experienced before. Dan had never been overtly mean to her, but he hadn't tried to make her feel good, either. He'd been stingy with compliments, and when he finally gave them, there was always a kicker at the end. "Love this lasagna, babe, but I think you're puttin' on a few pounds of ravioli, if you know what I mean." She shuddered, hearing his voice as if he were right behind her. She felt embarrassed as always that it had taken her so long to wake up and see her marriage for what it was. Maybe if she hadn't been so young—

"What's wrong?"

She snapped back to the present and saw that Jarred had finished carving and was trying to give her her plate. She took it quickly, hoping she hadn't been zoned for too long. "Nothing," she said. "I guess I'm just tired."

"Right." Jarred nodded, but he kept looking at her. She could see the concern in his eyes, which was exactly her point. He was too nice. Too considerate. He made her wish for things that could never be. She'd already had to rearrange her dreams once. She didn't want to do it again.

He finished fixing his own plate, and as she gave herself a very healthy serving of stuffing, she asked, "How come you're not married?"

He dropped his fork, but that was the only sign that she'd surprised him with her question. "I haven't met the right woman, I guess," he answered, paying more attention to his meat than her.

"What would the right woman be like?"

He took a bite of turkey, and even managed to swallow without choking. Then, after a healthy swig of wine, he leaned back. "Well, I'm not sure I know."

"You must have some things that are must-haves."

"Sure, sure," he said. "She'd have to be—"

"Pretty?"

He smiled. "It wouldn't hurt, but that's not what I was going to say."

"Sorry. I'll be patient."

"Hmm. Patience. That's a good one, too."

"Come on, tell me what you were going to say."

"She'd have to be nice."

Beth blinked. "Nice?"

"Yeah. Nice. You know. Nice."

She hid her smile behind her wineglass. "Yes, that's important."

"It is."

"I'm agreeing with you."

"Then why are you smiling like that?"

She put her glass down, not really shy about showing him her delight. "I'm smiling because I think that may just be the best answer I ever heard to that question."

His head cocked slightly to the right. "Are you having fun with me, Mrs. Cochran?"

"No, not even a little bit. I'm very serious."

"What about you?"

"Hmm?"

"What would your perfect man be like?"

She almost said "You," but caught herself just in time. Blushing furiously, she busied herself with her food. "Nice works for me, too," she said. "Kind."

"Handsome?"

She shrugged. "That's a bonus, but not at all required."

"Smart?"

"Also a plus."

"Sexy?"

"I find that if a man is nice and kind and smart, he's usually sexy."

"Nope, I don't buy it. Sam's nice, kind and smart."

"True. And if I were closer to his age, I'd find him quite sexy."

"You're cheating."

"I'm not," she said. "Besides, it was my question. You just didn't want to reveal too much, so you turned the tables."

He chuckled, making her stomach tighten, just like always. "I'm not trying to be evasive. Honest."

"Really?"

He nodded, his smile fading into a look of quiet contemplation. "I'll know her," he said softly. "I'll know her when I meet her."

Beth felt a little chill run down her spine. He hadn't met her yet. That's what he was saying. He had an ideal woman, and it wasn't her.

She smiled as warmly as she could, forcing any trace of her disappointment to the back of her mind, away from his perceptive gaze. "I know you'll find her someday, Jarred."

"I hope so," he said. "Being here—"

"Yes?"

He gave a quick shake of his head. "It's just, I haven't really been around a family before."

"That's right," she said. "Of course not."

"I like it."

"Do you?"

"Not everything," he said. "I'm pretty used to getting the bathroom when I need it."

"And finding your book exactly where you'd left it."

"Sleeping in on Sunday."

"Not having to make up a bedtime story every night," she said, the bad feeling she'd had only moments ago dissipating, not because she wasn't still smarting, but because she realized how absurd it was to get bent out of shape about him. It wasn't as if they were lovers or anything. The attraction was there, but that wasn't anything more than hormones. And, yes, he was the nicest guy she'd ever met, but that's just because she hardly met any guys. She'd been married at seventeen, and she'd never been out with any other man. She hadn't even had male friends.

"No," Jarred said. "I don't know about that one."

"Which one?"

"Having to make up a bedtime story."

"You like that? Jarred, I've heard some of your stories. You'd better be glad there are no copyright police around here, or your behind would be in the slammer."

"Hey, I never claimed to be original."

"On the contrary. Combining *Alice in Wonderland* and *Star Trek: The Next Generation* was highly original."

"They liked it, though, didn't they?"

She nodded. "They sure did."

He sighed and went on with his meal. She poured him some more wine, then she, too, concentrated on the terrific food. But her thoughts...they were stuck in a groove between bedtime stories and rooftop kisses, and they didn't budge until after dessert.

JARRED STOOD IN the hallway. He'd intended on walking into the twins' room and giving them the latest installment of his version of Galaxy Man Saves the World. But Beth was already there, tucking Karen in. Debbi had gotten her kiss, and now the three Cochran women sat in the dim glow of the Little Mermaid night-light.

"Mom?"

"Yes, honey?"

"Are you going to stay here this weekend?"

"Yes."

"And, Mom?"

"Yes, Karen?"

"Is he going to be here, too?"

"Uh-huh."

"What about next week?" Karen continued. "Will you be here next week?"

"As far as I know, I'll be home. But I might get another job. You remember I told you that it was hard to be sure when I'd have to work."

"Well," Karen said, "is Jarred going to be here next week?"

"Sweetie, I already told you that, too. He's going to be here for several weeks. He's helping with the house."

"Mom?"

Beth turned so that she could stroke both girls' blond heads at the same time. The twins looked incredibly small and fragile underneath the comforters, and yet Jarred knew they had the same inner strength as their mother.

"Mom?" Debbi repeated. "Mom, will Jarred stay here forever?"

"No, sweetheart."

"Why not?"

"Because he lives somewhere else. As soon as the house is finished, he'll be going back home."

"Why?"

"Because he has his own home and his own life."

"Doesn't he like us enough to stay?"

"He likes us a great deal, especially you two. And that won't stop when he leaves."

"Mom?" Karen asked.

"Yes?"

"If we ask him, can he stay?"

"No, love. And you mustn't ask him. That would make him uncomfortable, and we don't want to do that, do we?"

"No, but—"

"Promise me, girls."

"I promise," Debbi mumbled.

"I promise," Karen repeated.

"Thank you. Now, no talking. You go right to sleep."

"Mom?"

"Yes, Karen," Beth said as she stood up.

"We know who he is."

"You do?"

"Uh-huh," Karen said, but it ended in a long yawn.

"Who is he?"

"It's a secret."

"Okay, sweetie." She kissed Karen on the forehead, and then moved over to kiss Debbi, but Jarred didn't see that. He hurried down the hall to the attic stairs and climbed them as quietly as he could. Then he shut his door behind him.

It only took about five minutes to get ready for bed,

but it took him hours to fall asleep. He just couldn't stop thinking. About the girls. About Caleb. The house. But he always came back to Beth. Simply Beth.

CHAPTER FOURTEEN

THE FIRST THING HE SAW when he woke up was Galaxy Man.

The comic was on the floor, right next to his bed. Someone, and he was guessing it wasn't Beth, had been in his room. Had left him a present. A unique present at that.

He sat up, stretched, cursed his lower back, then bent forward to pick up the comic. Just as his hand touched the cover, his hazy brain made the connection. He lifted the comic, studying it hard, making sure he really saw what he thought he saw.

Galaxy Man, while much more muscular and, of course, two-dimensional, shared a lot of features with Jarred. The hair. The eyes. The height. Even his nose and the superhero's were shaped similarly. Hell, they could be twins. If he were a cartoon character, that is. Or if Galaxy Man were real.

Which, he now understood, was exactly what the twins believed. He sat back on the bed and read the comic from cover to cover. He'd forgotten some of the G-man's superpowers, particularly the ability to freeze his foes with a point of his finger. Actually, he felt kind of flattered. If he couldn't be mistaken for Harrison Ford, then Galaxy Man wasn't half-bad.

Chuckling, he carefully put the comic away in his suitcase as he thought about the possibilities of this revelation. He could make things interesting around here, that's for sure. Of course, he'd have to tell them the truth. But not yet. There was no hurry, right?

He shook his head, remembering how they'd reacted to him that first day at the auction. They'd believed completely that he could rebuild their house in a whirlwind of blurry lines and accelerated time. Hadn't they figured out yet that he worked at the pace of a normal human?

He grabbed his clothes and his toiletry kit and headed for the john. It was, miraculously, empty, although telltale signs that children had occupied the territory only moments before hung in the air. And on the floor. Their towels, dropped in terry-cloth puddles, lay right in front of the double sink. Ariel, the mermaid he'd become startlingly aware of in the last couple of weeks, sat in the soap dish. Rugrats toothbrushes had been discarded on the counter. He spied something behind the commode and bent to retrieve it. It was the head of a doll. Just the head. He put it on the counter with a little shudder, hoping someone would come up with a body.

He got in the shower, grateful that all the hot water wasn't gone. He thought about the girls and their mistaken impression of him. The towels they wore like capes. The crazy questions they asked him, and of course the stories he told each night. It cracked him up, but he also realized they were impressionable kids, and he should talk to Beth and ask her advice on how to handle this.

But who would give him advice about how to handle Beth?

Damn, but he wanted her. He'd thought it would grow easier, but it had only grown harder, pardon the pun. Her scent had seeped inside him, her voice replayed in his mind, and the way she looked—that was a fixed image now, down to the finest detail. What he hadn't seen in person, he'd conjured, making his nights far too restless.

If he didn't pick up the pace at the house, he'd never make it to the finish without doing something stupid. He'd thought about hiring extra help several times, but he'd hesitated. Not anymore. He would call the construction company here in town on Monday. Get himself a good crew. He would fulfill his end of the bargain, but he'd do it faster. She'd probably balk at the cost, but there was no way he was going to let her talk him out of it. The longer he stayed here, the closer he came to crossing the line. That wasn't smart for him or for her. He wasn't going to stick around. He didn't want a long-term commitment. He wasn't the kind of guy a family should count on.

And Beth? Hell, she was too vulnerable for her own good. Too soft, too beautiful. Too trusting.

He knew beyond doubt that if he pressed, he could get her into his bed. It would be incredible, there was no doubt about that, either. But the consequences would be too high. He'd lose all the points he was making by finishing the house, plus about a thousand more.

So the only thing to do was finish the house, by whatever means necessary, and leave this place, this state, forever. It was the only thing that made sense.

That decided, he finished rinsing his hair and shifted into work mode.

Twenty minutes later, he was downstairs, and he heard the girls in the kitchen. It was still early, just past six, and he didn't believe Beth was up yet. Caleb was probably still sleeping, too.

He smiled and crept toward the kitchen, eavesdropping the moment he could make out their voices.

"...tell. You're not supposed to have cookies before breakfast."

"Who says?"

"Mom, that's who."

That was Karen's voice. So Debbi must be the one with her hand in the cookie jar.

"Mom isn't even up."

"So?"

"So, she won't know."

"Yes, she will," Karen said. "She always knows."

"Not if you don't tell her."

"We should have some cereal," Karen said. "She won't mind that."

He got to the doorway, holding himself flat against the wall so they wouldn't see him. He heard Debbi chomping on her cookie, then he heard the scrape of a chair.

"I told you it would taste good," Debbi said thickly, through chocolate chips and crumbs.

"If we get in trouble, I'm telling Mom it was your idea."

"We won't get in trouble if you just be quiet and eat the cookie."

That's when he made his move. He didn't just walk into the kitchen, he *bounded*. Puffing up his chest, he leapt like a crazed gazelle, whipped out his index finger to point at the girls, and cried, "Freeze!"

They did. Immediately. Debbi had one foot off the ground, but she didn't lose her balance.

Karen was mid-chomp and her mouth hung open. It was wise not to look there.

He eyed the girls, arching one brow dramatically, keeping his finger pointed at them accusingly. They teetered, and their eyes got very, very wide, but he had to give them credit. When they froze, they stayed frozen.

"Who said you could eat cookies for breakfast?" he intoned, lowering his voice and trying like heck to sound like James Earl Jones.

Neither girl answered. It took him a few seconds to realize he hadn't un-frozen them. He switched hands, pointing now with his left index finger. That did the trick. Debbi's foot came down, and Karen's mouth shut.

"You *are* Galaxy Man," Debbi said.

"I knew it," Karen whispered.

"We'll talk about that another time," he said, keeping in character as much as he could. "Right now, you need to go wash up, and then you need to eat a healthy breakfast."

The girls, staring at him with unblinking, awed gazes, nodded in unison. Karen put the uneaten half of her cookie right on the floor, never taking her eyes off him.

They backed out of the kitchen, shuffling on little bare feet, their nightshirts brushing their ankles. He doubted very much that either girl would ever have another cookie for breakfast.

As soon as they were in the hallway, he exhaled. It wasn't easy being a superhero. But it was kinda fun.

He chuckled again as he got out the eggs and the

milk and started fixing breakfast. Kids. They were just too much.

BETH HEARD THE LAUGHTER long before she actually walked into the kitchen. The twins were standing on their chairs, pointing their fingers at Caleb, who stared at them as if they'd both gone plumb loco. But it was Jarred's rich, low laughter that made her go all soft. "What in the world?" she asked.

The girls turned to face her, swinging their pointed fingers right at her nose. They laughed hysterically, looked at Jarred, and laughed some more.

Jarred shrugged. "It's way too complicated. Trust me. Just have your coffee and I'll explain later."

She shook her head, wondering what had gotten into everybody and wishing she'd come downstairs sooner. Jarred handed her a mug of coffee, and then he held her chair for her, just like a real gentleman.

She sat, loving the morning gift of being served. Being treated like a princess. Doubly so, in that it was a passing thrill that would be gone far too quickly.

"Those two are nuts," Caleb said. "You ought to lock them up in the loony bin."

"This *is* the loony bin, Caleb," she said. "Didn't you know that?"

"Ha-ha. Very funny."

She reached over and grabbed her son's cheeks, then gave him a very loud kiss right on the mouth. He reared back, wiping his mouth dramatically with the back of his hand and issuing a long, lyrical "Ewwwwww."

She didn't care one whit. "Ladies," she said, turning to the twins. "Sit."

"But—"

"Sit."

They sighed heavily, then they sat, each making a very big production of the process.

"What do you want in your omelet?" Jarred asked.

She looked over at him, standing by the stove, spatula in one hand, coffee mug in the other. The sun decided to break through the morning clouds right then and made him look shimmery and golden and otherworldly. That last part was true, at least. He was definitely from another world. Something other than Mars. With his smoldering good looks, she'd put her money on Venus.

"I've got tomatoes," he said. "Onions. Ham. Green pepper and, of course, gummy bears."

She grinned as his cute little comment stirred up a hornet's nest of complaints that he hadn't offered the twins any gummy bear omelets.

"He was joking, you pea brains," Caleb said.

"Artichoke head," Karen shot back.

"Onion butt!" Debbi added.

Beth just smiled as she took another sip of her hot coffee. She felt wonderful. For the first time all week, she'd slept the whole night. It probably had something to do with the fact that she'd been almost as exhausted as when the twins were infants. She'd always heard renovations were tough on the homeowners, but no one could have prepared her for this. Or for Jarred.

"So, what's it going to be?" Jarred prompted.

"Ham and cheese, if you've got it."

"Comin' right up." He turned to the counter, and with the same kind of purposeful grace he employed when he shingled the roof or plastered the tile, he built her a three-egg omelet. He didn't waste a motion or break his rhythm. The whole routine should have been put to music.

"What are we gonna build today, Jarred?" Debbi asked. "Can't we do our bedroom?"

"Honey," Beth said, grabbing the half-full glass of milk that was far too close to Debbi's elbow for comfort. "Honey, I told you. We need to do the guest rooms first. Our rooms come last."

"I know. But don't we get to stay in the guest rooms if there're no guests?"

"Only while your real room is being fixed."

"So why don't we fix our real rooms first?"

"Because we need to spend our time and energy on things that can bring in some money."

Debbi thought about that for a few minutes. "If you don't give me an allowance for two months, can we do our real room first?"

Beth wished she could say yes. Three people were getting the short end of the stick in this deal, and they were all under ten. But she had to keep putting eggs in the fridge and milk on the table. "We'll see," she said.

Debbi's look said that she understood what "we'll see" meant. But to her credit, she let it go.

"Are you ready?" Jarred said, standing with his back to her, hiding his culinary creation. Of course, with those shoulders, he could have hidden a whole restaurant.

"I'm more than ready," she said. "I'm famished."

"Drum roll, if you please," he said. When no one did anything, he shot a look at Caleb. "Uh, drum roll?"

Caleb rolled his eyes instead.

Beth supplied the real sound effect, and as soon as the girls understood what she was doing, they took over. Beating an uneven tempo on the Formica table, and trying to roll their *R*s, they sounded awful, but at least they were loud.

"Ta-da!" Jarred said, whirling around. He lowered his masterpiece down so she and the kids could see.

"Oh, Jarred," Beth said, only exaggerating a bit. "It's gorgeous." She turned to the girls. "Debbi, Karen, look at how wonderful it is." Then she nudged Caleb in the side. "Isn't that something?"

"It's eggs," Caleb said, his voice as dry as the Sahara.

"Ah, but what eggs. Has there ever been such perfection? Fluffy, but not too fluffy. Golden with just a hint of brown on the edges. The ham and cheese proportioned as if by Solomon himself."

Everyone stared at her, including Jarred. She grinned. "So I got a little carried away. Sue me."

Jarred smiled, putting the plate carefully in front of her. "I liked it," he said. "I think I'll hire you to do the PR for my company."

"You're on," she said. Then she took the first bite, and there was no way she could hold back the yummy noises. She moaned, sighed, chewed. "There's one condition," she said after she'd swallowed. "Only you have to pay me in omelets."

"It's a deal," he agreed, slipping into his seat.

She ate for a while, unwilling and quite possibly unable to stop until she'd practically inhaled half the eggs. Then she forced herself to slow down. To sip some coffee. When she smiled at Jarred, she saw he was staring at her, a kind of funny, crooked smile on his lips. "What?"

"You're really pretty."

"Thank you."

"I mean it."

"I'm flattered," she said. Not to mention flustered. But she could feel storm clouds brewing next to her. She quirked her head toward Caleb, and Jarred gave her a small nod of understanding. "Hey, listen up, everyone," she said, changing the subject as quickly as she could. "I've got an idea."

"What?" Karen and Debbi asked simultaneously.

Caleb didn't say a thing. He just pushed his plate away, his breakfast half-eaten.

"How about we all play hooky today? Let's go somewhere. Into Casper, or out into the mountains."

"Yay!

"Yes, yes, yes, yes!"

So much for the girls. She looked at Caleb, and to her surprise, his look of fierce unhappiness had transformed into one of mere boredom. In the world according to Caleb, that was practically like being ecstatic.

Finally, her gaze went to Jarred. He mouthed, "You sure?"

She nodded.

"I know some places around here," he said. "Most gorgeous country in the world. We can go hiking at the foot of the Bighorn Mountains. Take a picnic." He looked at Caleb. "Maybe we can even play a game of catch, huh?"

Caleb shrugged.

"And we can collect leaves and pretty rocks," Beth added. "Right, girls?"

"Can we find some bears?" Karen asked.

"I wanna ride up front," Debbi shouted.

"You can't. Mom's gonna ride up front," Karen said. "Right?"

"We'll see who rides where when we're ready. But we're not leaving until you've all eaten your breakfast and we've all cleaned the kitchen."

"That's not like any hooky I know," Caleb said.

"It's the only hooky you're gonna get." Beth rubbed the top of his head, which she knew drove him crazy. "Eat up, cowboy. We're gonna have us an adventure."

She finished her own omelet, listening as the girls debated what to wear, what toys to bring and how many thousands of leaves they were going to collect. Jarred got himself another cup of coffee, then relaxed again in his chair, taking it all in. It must be odd for a single man, she thought. For someone so unused to the madness of a gaggle of kids. And yet he handled it like an old pro. Maybe growing up at the orphanage had made him better able to share with others. Or maybe it was just that he was lonely in Houston, and this was a nice change of pace. Temporary, but nice.

"Mom."

"Mom!"

She looked at her little angels. "Yes?"

"I think someone's here," Karen said.

Caleb shot out of his seat, but she caught him by the tail of his shirt just as he was about to make his getaway. "Sit down, Speedy Gonzales. I'll answer it."

He groaned as he slunk back to his seat. Beth got up, wondering who it could be. Sam, probably. He'd taken to dropping by on a regular basis, mostly to check up on Jarred, but also to make sure she and the kids were okay. She was glad he was here early so he could join them for breakfast. She had a feeling Sam would like that very much.

On her way to the door, she picked up a bandanna, a tennis shoe and a Barbie with no head. She stuck them in a box as she reached for the knob and pulled. When she turned back, the door was open, but instead of Sam's smiling face, she stood toe to toe with her husband, Dan.

CHAPTER FIFTEEN

SHE'D BEEN GONE about five minutes when Jarred realized something was wrong. The kids didn't seem concerned. They were still deep in conversation about their upcoming adventure. At least the girls were. Caleb was listening to them, or at least he was looking their way. His eyes seemed glazed, as if his mind was far, far away.

Jarred got up, wondering now who could be at the door and why Beth hadn't come back. He headed for the living room and almost tripped over Debbi, who suddenly shot past him. Before he reached the kitchen door, he heard her high-pitched squeal. "Daddy!"

Daddy? Caleb and Karen scrambled out of their seats, almost bowling him over in their rush to see their father.

Had he made plans to visit? Beth hadn't said a word. In fact, Jarred was under the impression she didn't expect to see him again.

He reached the living room, hanging back by the wall as he watched the rough-and-tumble welcome. The kids were so excited, they could barely speak. Jarred had never seen Caleb like this, grinning so hard his eyes almost disappeared. But Beth didn't share their enthusiasm. Her lips pressed together in a tight line of disapproval. Her brows furrowed with concern, and she had her arms crossed over her chest defensively.

Dan was not an expected guest, that was clear.

Jarred looked him over. He was a nice-looking guy. Dark haired, tanned enough to worry a dermatologist. He wasn't very tall, but he was broad. He worked out. And he wanted people to know it. He'd taken off his sport coat to show off his one-size-too-small yacht club T-shirt. But what really bothered Jarred was that his smile didn't reach his eyes, even when he had Debbi and Karen hanging on to his legs. Jarred couldn't be sure if it was knowing something about the man that made him dislike him on sight, or if it was a legitimate gut feeling. Either way, he wanted him gone.

Dan finally looked over to where Jarred stood. The fact that a strange man was in his wife's house at seven-thirty in the morning didn't seem to bother him. He just nodded, as if they were acquaintances meeting at a bus stop.

"Dan, that's Jarred McCoy. He's helping me with the house."

"Yeah? Great. It looks like it's coming right along."

"It's slow," Beth said, her voice so tight Jarred barely recognized it. "But we'll get there."

"Hey, listen. Can we go into the kitchen for a minute? We need to talk."

"Don't you want to talk to the kids first? They've missed you terribly."

He smiled at the girls, patting them absently on the head, then winked at Caleb. "You bet. Where shall we go?"

"My room's back there," Caleb said, pointing to his end of the house.

"Then that's where we're headed."

Caleb led his father and sisters past the jumble of boxes and supplies in the living room. As they passed Jarred, Debbi and Karen jumped up and down, flanking Dan on either side.

"This is our daddy!" Karen said by way of introduction.

Not to be outdone, Debbi bounced over to Jarred and announced, "This is our Jarred!"

Dan paused. For the first time, he really checked Jarred out, starting at the top and working his way down. When he finished, he stuck out a thick hand. "How you doing?"

Jarred accepted the greeting, taking the opportunity to study the man. "Fine, thanks."

Then the parade passed, leaving Beth and Jarred in its wake.

"Surprised?" he asked, walking over to her. She hadn't moved at all.

"To say the least."

"Any idea why he'd show up like this?"

She shook her head, still staring at the doorway to the hall, as if expecting Dan to pop back around the corner. "The only thing I can think of is that he's brought the final divorce papers. Although there's no reason for him to do that in person. The attorneys have been handling everything."

"Maybe he wanted to speed things up?"

"I can't imagine why. But I guess I'll find out soon enough."

Jarred didn't say anything for a long while. He

didn't press her for conversation. But he hoped she knew she could talk to him if she wanted to.

"I'd better go clean the kitchen," she said.

"I'll help."

"You don't have to."

"I know." He followed her back into the kitchen, the remains of their rather exuberant meal spread out on the table and counter. He took his lead from her, gathering dishes, putting away food, mopping up spills. Every time he thought she was going to say something, she turned away. He didn't care for this feeling one bit. He wanted to help her, but how? What the hell did he know about her marriage?

It was none of his business. Not even the fact that Beth's hands trembled as she wiped them brusquely on the dish towel.

"I don't think we're going to make it to the mountains today," Beth said after the dishes were half-washed. "The kids, they'll want to stay with their father."

"Sure. Sure, no problem. I'll make myself scarce. I've been meaning to go out to see Sam. I'm overdue."

"No!" He heard the urgency in her voice even though she'd said the word so softly. "I mean, it's okay if you want to stay. You don't have to leave. You can if you want, though."

He smiled, putting his hand on the small of her back just to reassure her that he wasn't going anywhere. What he really wanted to do was to pull her into his arms and hold her tight until she stopped shaking, but that wouldn't help the situation. "No problem," he said. "I'll stay. I'll be right here."

Her back muscles didn't relax at all. "Maybe you

could just do something with the kids while Dan and I talk?''

"You got it."

She looked at him for the first time since they'd been in the kitchen. She seemed very young and very vulnerable, but the strength and determination that he'd come to admire so much were still there. A mite wobbly, but there. She'd protect her kids like the mama bear she was.

"Thank you."

"For what?" he asked, smiling as casually as he could.

She gave him a small upward quirk of the lips. Not quite a smile, but almost. "For the omelet."

He shrugged. "They were just eggs."

She turned away again, busying herself with the last of the dishes. Jarred's smile faded as he realized exactly what was going on. Not between Beth and Dan, but inside him. He'd grown to care about this woman, and this family. What happened to them mattered. A lot. For the first time since he'd lost his parents all those years ago, he'd let down his guard.

He heard Debbi's footfalls before she got to the doorway, and then he saw she wasn't alone. The whole gang had followed. Dan greeted him with a cool glance, then headed toward Beth. "Have a minute?"

She grabbed the dish towel and dried her hands. "Sure."

He looked back at the kids. "Mom and I need to talk, you guys. So why don't you go out and play?"

"I'll take them," Jarred said. He started to head outside, but Caleb stopped him.

"I don't want to go outside."

"Your folks need some privacy."

"So? That doesn't mean I have to go outside."

Jarred glanced at Beth, but she looked as if she had enough on her plate at the moment, so he switched gears. "Okay. Let's go to the living room. We'll have ourselves a powwow."

The girls seemed fine with the plan, but Caleb dawdled, looking at his father, then at his mother. Even Jarred could interpret his silent plea for them to get back together.

Jarred put his hand on Caleb's back and urged him out of the kitchen. Debbi went right to the front door and started pawing through a box. Karen plopped herself down next to her. Caleb hovered near the kitchen.

"Come on, kids. I've got a really spooky story."

Debbi was over in a flash, holding the body of a doll that he assumed belonged to the head upstairs. She didn't seem to mind that the doll was headless, which made him realize that the spooky story he'd planned on telling wasn't going to be nearly spooky enough.

Still, Caleb didn't move. He stared at the door, his shoulders tightly squeezed together in a posture of uneasy tension.

"Hey, buddy," Jarred called. "Come on over, okay?"

The boy shook his head. He wasn't going to budge. Jarred knew he could physically carry the nine-year-old with ease, but the resultant brouhaha wouldn't exactly give Beth the privacy she needed.

Well, if the mountain wouldn't come to Mohammed... "Come on girls. Let's go sit over by Caleb."

The three of them got up and regrouped right next to the kitchen door. Caleb was in the circle by default, but he didn't actually join them. He just stood there as if he was trying to see through the wall.

Jarred didn't know what else to do, so he started his story. At the last minute, he decided to use an episode from the *X-Files*, the one with the big flatworm, because he couldn't think of anything else. To his knowledge, none of Beth's kids watched the show, so he felt pretty safe.

But it wasn't easy. Not with Caleb standing like a statue, and the girls interrupting every three seconds. After a while, Jarred realized he could hear Beth and Dan. He couldn't make out the words, but he could tell there was one hell of an argument going on.

"Caleb," he said. "Come on, kiddo. Do you like it when people eavesdrop on you?"

"He's my father," Caleb said, as if that justified any action he might take.

"I know, but even fathers have some things they'd like to keep to themselves."

Caleb didn't acknowledge him in any way. The voices grew louder, the words becoming clear. Achingly clear.

"Oh, Dan." Beth's voice sounded shrill and desperate, even at this distance. "Can't you see how much he needs you?"

"Quiet down, Beth."

"I won't."

"I'm not abandoning him, for God's sake. He's my son."

"All he wants is to understand," she said. "To know you still love him."

"I do. But I can't take him right now. Julie and I are getting married."

"When?"

"Next month."

"Why the rush?"

"We're starting our own family. Julie's having a baby."

Caleb's head snapped back as if he'd been hit by lightning. Jarred was on his feet in a heartbeat, grabbing for the boy. He got him, but Caleb fought like a tiger. Jarred was afraid he was going to really hurt himself. He walked away from the connecting wall, the whole time saying, "You don't want to hear this, Caleb. You don't want to hear this."

As soon as he put the boy down, Caleb darted across the room again to stand as close as he could to the kitchen door. Jarred had to do something.

"Will you sign the goddamn papers?" Dan shouted, his voice reverberating through the thin walls.

Jarred knew it was too late. That Caleb and the girls had heard too much. Words that couldn't be taken back. Debbi was crying, the tears just rolling down her cheeks. Karen held her sister's hand as she squeezed her eyes shut tight. And Caleb. Caleb was white as a ghost.

Jarred swooped down, picking up the girls, one in each arm. They both instantly wrapped their arms around his neck, almost cutting off his air supply. He felt them struggle for position with their legs around his waist. "You guys hold on, okay?" Then he went to Caleb and moved between him and the wall. "We're leaving."

Caleb didn't respond in any way.

"Now."

He shifted the girls so they could hang on without his help. Once he was sure they were okay, he picked

Caleb up, holding him very tightly to his chest. Although the boy couldn't move his arms, he sure as hell could move his legs. He kicked Jarred over and over, wailing with all his might, screaming "No! No! No!" in a voice that Jarred wouldn't forget for the rest of his life.

Despite the screams and the kicks and the heaviness of the three children, Jarred got across the living room remarkably quickly. Then he was outside, walking away from the house, past the Ford Taurus parked in front, nearly choking as the girls squeezed his neck.

He didn't stop until he was a hundred yards away from the porch. Far enough so that no amount of shouting would find them. Then he crouched, letting the girls find the ground. He took in a great breath of air the second their arms slackened. What he didn't do was let go of Caleb.

He just kept holding on, even as he got to his knees so that he didn't tower over the kids. Debbi and Karen hugged him around his neck once more, only this time, they didn't cut off his windpipe. The four of them stayed like that for a long time. Jarred felt tears soak through his shirt as he tried his best to calm everyone down.

He felt pretty sure that the girls were reacting more to Caleb than to Dan and Beth's argument. But Caleb had just heard his worst fear come to life. His father was starting a new family. The old one wasn't good enough. It was undeniable proof that Dan hadn't come to his rescue at all.

Jarred rocked him back and forth, letting him cry. The pain was all too familiar. The grief all too real. Jarred wished like hell he didn't know that the hurt would last for the rest of Caleb's life. But it would.

"He still loves you, Caleb," Jarred said. "Lots of people have two families. They love them both the same. It happens all the time."

He didn't know if Caleb heard him, or if any of his words had gotten through, but after a while, the tears stopped flowing. Jarred let Caleb's arms go, and he jerked back, wiping his eyes and cheeks with his hands.

"You okay, kiddo?"

Caleb wouldn't look at him. "I'm fine."

"You sure?"

"What do you care? You don't really live here."

"I still care."

Caleb walked a few feet away to an old fence post. Debbi and Karen didn't move at all, but they'd stopped crying, too.

"Jarred?" Debbi asked.

"Yep?"

"Is daddy divorcing us?"

"Nope. That's not how it works. Even if your mom and dad get a divorce, they can never divorce you."

Debbi moved in front of him, and that stirred Karen to join her. As soon as they were together, they automatically held hands. He was grateful they had that small comfort.

"Why is Caleb crying?" Karen asked.

Before he could answer, Jarred heard the front door shut. He got to his feet quickly and turned to find Dan and Beth standing on the porch.

"Kids?" Beth called. "Come say goodbye to Daddy."

The girls looked at Jarred, and after he gave them a quick nod, they headed toward the house. Caleb didn't even turn around.

"Caleb?" Beth called again.

He kicked the fence post, staring a hole through the top of it. He wasn't about to say goodbye to his father. Not today.

Beth walked toward them, and as she grew near, Jarred could see that the kids weren't the only ones who'd been crying. She spared him the briefest glance, then pulled Caleb into her arms. He bucked for a moment, but only a moment. Then he flung his arms around her waist and buried his head against her tummy.

Jarred turned away. It was a personal moment, and he didn't want to intrude. But he wanted to tell Caleb how lucky he was. That his father might have disappointed him, but his mother was there, and she always would be.

Instead, he headed for the house. Dan was by the Ford, holding Karen in the crook of his arm while Debbi sat on the hood. He kept looking back over at Caleb and Beth. Jarred willed him to go to his son. To make things right, before it was too late and he could never make it right.

But that's not what happened. As Jarred stepped up on the porch, Beth let Caleb go. She went over to the car and helped Debbi get down. She took both girls by the hand and headed inside.

Dan took another long look at Caleb, who faced the other direction defiantly, and then he got in his car. The engine turned, intruding on the silence of the front yard. Even the crunch of dirt underneath the tires seemed out of place and rude.

Jarred felt little-girl fingers slip into his hand, and he took hold as the car disappeared down the long road. When it was all gone but the dust, Debbi pulled on him, tugging his hand until he looked down into her soft-green eyes. "You can fix it. You can make Daddy love us again. I know you can. Fix it, Galaxy Man. Do it now."

CHAPTER SIXTEEN

BETH LOOKED UP AT the soft knock on her door, but didn't get out of bed. It was probably one of the kids. After a day like today, it wouldn't surprise her at all if they couldn't sleep. She didn't think she would be able to. "Come in."

The door opened slowly. Jarred stood hesitantly outside, as if he were still debating his decision to come see her. "Hi."

She tried to smile, but it didn't work. Which wasn't fair. Jarred had been wonderful. He'd read the girls an entire Bobbsey Twins book, he'd fixed them all lunch, and bless him, he'd been there for Caleb. Today would have been infinitely harder if she'd had to face it on her own.

"I just wanted to make sure you were okay," he said. "I'll see you in the morning."

"No, it's okay. You don't have to leave."

He walked in, taking a quick look around before his gaze settled back on her. After a long moment, he said, "Want to talk?"

She shook her head. "I don't think so. But I'm also not sure I want to be alone."

"No problem. I'm really good at that. Sitting in a room and not talking, I mean."

"You are, huh?"

He nodded. "I did it all through school."

"It's an underrated skill," she said, wishing she knew if she wanted him to go or stay. But that decision seemed completely beyond her control.

Jarred still stood by the door, evidently debating the same thing. She probably should make him feel more comfortable. But screw it. He was on his own.

As if he'd sensed she was going to leave him to his own devices, he took a quick deep breath, then plunged in, surprising her completely by heading straight for the other side of the bed. She turned, amazed, as he plumped her pillows then sat down, pretty as you please, leaning his back against her headboard. Then he smiled as if he'd done this a hundred times before.

"Excuse me?" she said.

His answer was a pat on the bed, right next to him.

"What?"

"Come on. I don't have all night. Just get over here."

"What do you have in mind?"

"If you'll move your butt over here, I'll explain."

She almost argued. Almost. But the kindness in his eyes and the warmth of his smile won the very short battle. Not at all sure what she was in for, she scooted back until she sat right next to him. His arm moved behind her shoulders, making it far too easy to relax with a sigh, to lay her head in the crook of his neck.

"Much better," he said.

"Oh my, yes."

"Just one more thing," he said, bracing her as he leaned to his right. A second later, the light went out, leaving them in the dark. The only light was a shimmer of moonglow cascading through the window.

Then he was back, cradling her once more. "Close your eyes," he whispered.

"Jarred…"

"Just do it."

"All right, all right. Sheesh."

"Are they closed?"

"Yes."

"Okay then. We're ready."

"For what?"

"Once upon a time," he began.

"Jarred!"

"Hey, I've gotten really good at this, so just hush and listen." He cleared his throat, waited a dramatic second, then started again. "Once upon a time there lived a wee woman and her three itty-bitty children who were on a long sea voyage. They'd been on the ship for years, and all they'd seen of the world was the ocean around them and the sky above. It was a difficult voyage, because the captain wasn't trustworthy and there were so few other hands. But they kept sailing, doing their duty, making the best of a hard situation. Until one day, there came a great storm."

Beth couldn't believe he was telling her a bedtime story. Just like he did for the twins. But as he told her story, his fingers found her temple and he rubbed her skin in an idle circle. His voice soothed her and his touch melted her tension, and she began to understand why the girls insisted on this treat every night.

"The storm was so great," he continued in a gravelly whisper, "the ship that had carried the wee woman and her children for so long broke apart on a foreign shore. The captain had abandoned ship, the supplies were gone, everything that had been comfortable and familiar had been washed away. Except, of course, they had one another.''

He leaned his cheek on her head for a moment. ''The wee woman began working immediately. She found them shelter, and she found them food. In a remarkably short time, it was as if they'd always been on this strange shore. Now that they realized it was their new home, the wee woman had a plan to make her shelter larger, so other people who might get lost at sea could stay. And maybe, they'd even pay her for her trouble.''

''From your lips to God's—''

Jarred moved his finger to her mouth, cutting her off. ''You're supposed to listen,'' he said. ''So no comments from the peanut gallery, okay?''

She nodded, thinking he would move his hand away. Which he did, after a fashion. But not until the rough pad of his index finger slid slowly across her lips, making her forget more than what she'd been about to say. He erased the cautionary reminder that he was only a friend who was telling her this story to give her comfort after a hard day. That it didn't mean anything. That his touch was a friend's touch.

''And then the itty-bitty children found a carpenter one day,'' he went on in his dreamy way. ''They brought him to the shelter, and they made him very welcome. But the children, being so young, thought he was more than a carpenter. They thought he was a hero. They believed it so much, the wee woman began to believe it, too. But that was a mistake.''

His hand moved back to her lips in a preemptive strike, stopping her argument before she could form the first word. And this time, he didn't move his hand away. This time, he rubbed her lips slowly, back and forth. The effect rippled through her, all the way down her body.

"Even after the captain returned, reminding the wee woman about the long voyage, threatening the calm of the shelter, the carpenter couldn't help. He wanted to. But he was just a carpenter."

His hand stilled on the side of her face, caressing her cheek tenderly. "What the wee woman didn't realize was that she didn't need the carpenter. Because this family already had a hero. Someone who made her children safe. Who turned tears into laughter. Who taught them every day about strength and determination and love and respect. This hero had given them things the captain couldn't take away, ever. This hero even taught the carpenter more about what a family is than he'd ever known."

Beth reached up and took his hand in hers, holding it steady as she tried not to cry. But then he hugged her, and the tears started. Sad tears, frightened tears. Tears of exhaustion and worry. But they were also strong tears, grateful tears. "How does the story end?" she asked, her voice as rough as the pads of his fingers.

"Very happily," he said. "The children grew accustomed to the new shelter, and they learned to thrive there. And the wee woman continued to be a hero for her family, even though most people didn't recognize her for what she was."

Beth sniffed, wiping her cheek with her free hand. "What about the carpenter?"

She waited for his answer, sure he would tell her that the carpenter went back to his own town to continue the life he'd built for himself. But Jarred didn't answer her at all.

She moved his hand away and leaned forward so she could look at him. Even in the dark, with only the light from the moon, she saw that he hadn't answered her because he didn't know that part of the story.

She didn't, either. Not the ending, at least. But she knew what she wanted to happen on this page. She shifted on the bed, turning in his arms, meeting his gaze in the dark.

"We shouldn't," he said.

She put her fingers on his lips, quieting his doubts, and her own. And then she quieted him again, this time with a kiss.

Softly at first. A shared breath. The scent of him imprinting on her forever. Then pressure, insistent, heady. A flick of his tongue, a teasing nip to her bottom lip.

She groaned with abandon as his arm slipped under her knees. He lifted her as if she *were* that wee woman and put her on his lap, adjusting her perfectly for his next kiss.

His arms wrapped around her like the warmest blanket, his hands exploring her body through her clothes. She knew he felt her heat, he had to. She ran her hands through his clean dark hair, gripping him tightly as he slipped his tongue between her teeth.

From that moment on, she was his. She wanted him inside her, and she wanted him around her, and she let him lead her step by step...his hands grasping her shirt and lifting it over her head. His kisses on the flesh above the cups of her bra. Gentle fingers releasing the clasp, peeling back the material as if he were opening the most precious present.

She moaned as his lips found her breasts, and he

licked and suckled and teased her with his amazing mouth. Taking his time, stoking the flames coal by coal.

When she moved her hands to the buttons on her jeans, he stopped her. And he didn't undress her until he'd laid her flat on the bed, so he could see her in the moonlight.

His big hands had no trouble with her buttons, and when they were undone, he eased her pants down, taking her panties along for the ride.

When he'd slipped them off the final inch, he tossed the pants on the floor mindlessly as his gaze explored her naked body. He took his time, nodding in appreciation. Looking at her in a way that was completely foreign to her—with desire and awe. His mouth opened when he reached her breasts, and he took in a great breath.

"Now you," she said, getting up on her elbows, surprised at her comfort, her willingness to let him look at her like that. Anxious to see him in return.

"Wait. Don't move."

She stopped, and quicker than she ever could have believed it, he stripped right down to the skin, stepping onto the floor to shake off his jeans.

And there he stood in all his glory, the muscles of his chest forming the perfect V. His slender waist, his "innie" belly button and the narrow line of dark hair that led her gaze down.

She blinked as she saw how very well-proportioned his body was…everywhere. He stood before her, hard and ready. She forced her gaze back to his face, where she blushed at his knowing smile.

"Well?" he said.

"It's terrific," she teased. "Am I supposed to applaud?"

He rolled his eyes at her. "That's not what I meant," he said. "I was trying to give you an out."

"What do I want an out for?"

"I don't know. Maybe because we both know this is nuts."

"I wouldn't put it that way," she said. "No, wait. I would. But I don't care."

"Really?"

"Uh-huh."

He climbed up on the bed, and spreading his hands and knees, he moved right over her, until they were eye to eye, inches apart. "I'll tell you a secret," he said. "I wouldn't have minded the applause."

"I'll try to remember that."

"On the other hand, you'll probably want to hold the standing ovation for after."

"For after what?" she asked innocently.

"For after *this*," he said, closing the distance between them.

HE WOKE UP VERY EARLY in the morning, just as the first rays of the sun were coming through the window. Beth's arm was on his chest, her small hand flat and pale and pretty against his skin. He followed the line of her shoulder, lingering on the curve of her neck. God, she was so beautiful. So...

He looked away, fixing his gaze on the window. What had he done? He'd crossed the line, and here he was on the other side without a plan. *This* was why he'd kept his hands to himself—because he'd known what it would be like to wake up next to her. To see her sleep, the way her eyelashes fanned out on her cheeks. To feel her knee pressed gently against his thigh.

This was the thing he was most afraid of. Wanting this. Needing this.

It wasn't his. Not to keep.

Moving as carefully as he could, he lifted her hand from his chest and put it on the pillow as he slipped from the bed. He pulled the comforter up to her chin, hiding the perfect shoulder. Quietly, quickly, he found his clothes and he left her room, heading right for the bathroom and a shower.

The children hadn't been there yet this morning, but they'd left their mark the night before. An impossibly small sneaker. Pink stretchy hair bands. A piece of torn paper with the word *mine* on it.

He'd always claimed he hated the mess of kids. In his home, he knew where everything was, and he was never surprised by what he found in his bathroom. Here, nothing surprised him, which was quite a different thing altogether.

It was hard to believe, but the truth was, he didn't mind finding an errant shoe. Or the head of a Barbie doll. He actually got a kick out of it. He liked not knowing what he'd find. It woke him up in a way that nothing had before.

Jarred turned on the water, waited until it was warm, then climbed in the shower. He closed his eyes and wallowed in the heat and steam. But before he took the soap in his hand, he brought his fingers to his face. Her scent. Heady and warm and womanly, it made him hard with the memory of what they'd done the night before.

The way she'd loved him made him rethink sex altogether. He'd always liked sex. A lot. Too much, sometimes, for his own good. But he'd never experienced anything or anyone like Beth. All he'd cared about was making her feel good. That was his whole goal. And what he'd gotten for his trouble was the most satisfying night of his life. It confused the hell out of him.

But he could worry about that mystery later. Right now, he had a more pressing problem: what to do next.

Of course, he would finish the house. He'd given his word. But starting Monday, he was going to get help. Professional help. He couldn't afford to stay any longer than necessary. He saw that with a clarity that stunned him. Not that he didn't want to stay. As crazy as it sounded, the thought of being a part of this family, of sleeping with Beth every night forever appealed to him as nothing had before. But that wouldn't be fair to Beth, would it?

Even as the idea of forever enticed him, he knew forever wasn't his destiny. He was a short-term lease, not a thirty-year mortgage, and that was just the truth. He knew it. Everyone in his company knew it. Beth knew it, whether she wanted to admit it or not.

And Sam, the old bastard, he knew it, too. He'd wanted to teach Jarred a lesson. Okay, so he got it. He understood now about trust and about faith. He had no illusions about the kind of man Beth deserved, and the kind of man he was, and how they were very different things.

He wished it could be another way. But that would be like wishing he was really Galaxy Man. Stupid. Stupid and sad.

He got the soap and the washcloth and he started scrubbing his body hard. He wanted the scent of her gone. Every trace, every hint that she'd made love with him.

But it didn't seem to matter how long he washed or how hard he scrubbed, he could still smell her, still feel the trace of her fingers across his back. Her voice echoed in his head, gasping and crying in her release.

It wasn't fair. He'd go crazy, remembering like this. He couldn't have her. And she was too vulnerable right now to see how wrong he was for her, so he had to be strong enough for both of them.

His laughter sounded shallow, bouncing off the tile walls. How in hell was he supposed to be strong, when he wanted her so damn much? When he knew she would say yes if he asked? Dammit, how was he going to say no when *she* asked *him?*

Once again, Sam had put a decision in his lap. He could do what felt good, or he could do what was right. The right choice would cost him a hell of a lot more than just a car this time.

This time, hearts were at stake. A wee woman and her itty-bitty children. They'd been bruised enough. They didn't need a carpenter to make things worse.

CHAPTER SEVENTEEN

THE FIRST THING BETH SAW when she woke up was the empty space where Jarred had slept. The depression was still in the pillow, but as she ran her hand over the pillow cover, she realized he'd been gone for a while. Long enough, certainly, for his warmth to dissipate.

Even though it was for the best that he'd left, she was disappointed. Expectation had awakened her, and she realized she must have been dreaming about him. About last night.

She pulled the covers up to her chin and closed her eyes, letting her mind's eye recall each tantalizing detail. He'd completely surprised her. Not that he'd done anything so out of the ordinary, but that he'd done everything so extraordinarily well. His touch, his kiss, his body. How could she have gone so long without understanding what making love was supposed to be? Her naiveté astounded her. But then, she'd only been with one man. And Dan, it turned out, was not the high benchmark when it came to lovers.

She'd only been thirteen when she met him. God, she'd been so flattered by his attention, and then when her parents took such a shine to him, it was like the icing on the cake. She'd never looked back. He'd been her everything.

They'd married right after high school, and it hadn't seemed unusual to her that Dan discouraged her from seeing her friends. She'd thought it was a sign of his love for her.

It had taken her a long time to wake up. To realize her relationship with Dan was deeply flawed. That their marriage wasn't normal or healthy. And then it had taken her even longer to finally give up. To realize she couldn't change him. The only thing she could change was herself.

During all those years with him, she'd never felt like she had last night. Dan had never focused on her the way Jarred had. Dan cared about his own satisfaction. If she found pleasure along the way, so much the better, but it wasn't really necessary. With Jarred... He'd taken her places she'd never been. Never dreamed of. My God, she'd climaxed more in one night with him than in all the nights she'd been with Dan put together!

But that wasn't even the best part. No man had ever treated her with the kind of respect that Jarred showed her. No one had ever taken the time to see who she was, let alone care. No one had ever reached the unique person that lived inside her. Until Jarred.

She supposed it wasn't fair to blame Dan. Neither of them had known better. The only thing she cared about now was how he treated the children. That he was starting another family worried her deeply. She just didn't know if Dan was mature enough to see past his own selfishness.

That was another area where Jarred came through like a champ. He was the least selfish man she'd ever met. The way he cared about her kids...

She smiled. It was late. She should get up. Well, maybe just a few more minutes.

She could still smell his scent in her sheets. Musky and masculine, the fragrance seemed to seep inside her and stir all sorts of interesting feelings. Oh, my.

No. She couldn't go there. She had a full day ahead, and the kids really needed her attention. Hanky-panky wasn't on the agenda. Besides, as glorious as it had been, it was still just a one-night thing. A reaction to a horrible day.

Doing it again wouldn't be wise, because Jarred was the kind of man she could grow used to. He'd never led her to believe, in any way, that he wanted a relationship with her, sexual or otherwise. Last night had just happened. She wasn't sorry. How could she be sorry?

She opened her eyes, not really wanting to see the clock but looking at it, anyway. It was almost nine, unspeakably late. The kids must have been up for hours. But of course, Jarred had fed them. She had no doubt about that.

No longer able to delay the inevitable, she climbed out of bed and headed for the shower. It was time to put last night to rest and get on with today.

WHEN SHE GOT DOWNSTAIRS, she found evidence that breakfast had been eaten. The dishes were in the sink, the coffee hot in the carafe and the syrup still on the table along with a lone place setting for her. "Hello?" she called out. "Kids? Jarred?"

No answer. She went to the living room, but that was empty. Peeking outside, she didn't find any of them in the front yard. She went back through the house to Caleb's room. A few feet from the door she heard voices.

Voices that made her slow down to a crawl.

"It doesn't mean he doesn't love you," Jarred said, his voice as kind as it had been last night in her bed. "No one can ever take your place. You're his kids, and you always will be, no matter how many other children he has."

"Why does he want to live with those children and not us?" Debbi asked.

Beth's breath caught, but she forced herself to let it out. To form an easy smile. To walk as if she wasn't facing the most difficult conversation of her life. She found them all together, Jarred sitting on the bed with Debbi on one side and Karen on the other. Caleb sitting on the corner of his desk. They looked so miserable, her heart squeezed tight. "'Morning."

Jarred gave her a sympathetic nod. "Hi. We were just talking."

"I heard," Beth said. "Can I join you?"

"Sure," Jarred said. "How about you two sitting right there on the floor and letting your mom sit next to me?"

The girls slid off the bed and plopped on the ground. They hadn't changed from their pajamas yet. Or combed their hair. Caleb was dressed, though. He had on his jeans and the same T-shirt he'd worn yesterday, which wasn't like him. He never liked to wear the same shirt twice.

Jarred looked as if he'd showered and shaved. He was in carpenter pants and a white T-shirt, and she thought again about his story. He denied being anything more than a carpenter, but she didn't believe it. He was more than that. Much more.

She sat down next to him and looked at her sad troupe. They hadn't really talked yesterday. The wounds had been too fresh. But today it was important to talk. To get it all out.

"Debbi, honey. Karen. Caleb. Remember how we talked about the divorce? Remember what I told you?"

"That you and Daddy didn't want to live together anymore," Karen said.

Debbi nodded. "That he was still our daddy, even if he lived in another house."

Caleb kicked the side of the desk. "You said he still loved us."

"He does still love you," Beth said. "He'll always love you."

"But he doesn't want us."

Beth wished she knew what to do. It felt as if anything she told them would break their hearts. "He doesn't want to live with *me*, sweetheart. Daddy and I fell out of love, and he fell in love with a new lady. He wants to live with her now."

Jarred found her hand and gave it a firm squeeze. "I'd better go start on the banister," he said. "I'll leave you guys to talk."

Beth held his hand steady. "You don't have to go."

He shook his head. "This is family business. I don't want to intrude."

She tried to catch his gaze, but he didn't look at her. He just ruffled Debbi's hair on his way out the door. She missed him immediately. Just feeling him next to her had given her strength.

"We were wrong about Jarred, Mommy," Karen said after he'd gone.

"Wrong?"

She nodded, her bottom lip quivering and her eyes glistening with tears. "We thought he was Galaxy Man, but he wasn't. He's just a nice man."

"I'm sure he didn't mean to disappoint you."

"I could have told you he wasn't Galaxy Man," Caleb said bitterly. "There's no such thing."

"There is, too," Debbi said.

"Is not. Only babies would believe something that stupid."

"Caleb," Beth said, warning him to knock it off with her tone.

He shot her an angry look, then went back to staring at the floor.

"We can talk about Jarred another time," she said. "Right now, I want to talk about Daddy. I want you to ask me any questions you have. Tell me anything you want."

Debbi stood and climbed onto the bed next to Beth. "When is Daddy's new baby coming?"

"In a few months."

"Will we get to see it?"

"I'm sure you will. The baby will be your half brother or sister."

"Really?" Debbi asked, obviously intrigued by the idea.

"Uh-huh."

"Daddy won't want us to see the new baby," Caleb said. "He doesn't want us around, or haven't you been listening?"

"Caleb. That's not true."

"It is so. I heard him. He said it."

"He didn't mean it. He was angry with me, not you."

Caleb looked at her, only this time his gaze wasn't just angry. It was full of pain and tears and confusion. "What did you do to him? Why'd you make him stop loving you?"

Beth forced her own tears back. She gave Debbi a tight hug, then she got up and went to her son. "Caleb?"

He wouldn't look at her.

"Honey, I need you to listen to me."

"I'm here," he mumbled.

She reached under his chin and lifted his head until she caught his gaze. "It's really difficult when mommies and daddies stop loving each other. But it's no one's fault. The one thing that hasn't changed, and will never change, is that your daddy and I love you very much. Even when we're not with you, we still love you."

He tried to move his head, but she held him firm, forcing him to keep looking into her eyes. She felt him tremble, saw his lips quiver, and then the first tear fell.

"Oh, baby," she said as she wrapped her arms around him tight.

He cried then. Cried as he hadn't for a very long time. Great racking sobs that shook his whole body. She rocked him back and forth, back and forth. She felt Debbi and Karen come up behind her, and they got on either side, grabbing hold of her. She moved her hands down to their little backs, bringing them into the circle.

The four of them cried and rocked until there were no more tears.

It took a long, long time.

JARRED STOPPED WORKING when he saw them come out of Caleb's bedroom. He sat halfway up the staircase, removing the loose banister rungs.

It must have been a rough talk. The whole family looked as if they'd been through the wringer. They all had red-rimmed, puffy eyes, and no one had a smile.

Karen disappeared into the living room and Caleb headed outside. Debbi walked over to the staircase and looked up at him. "Can I go upstairs?"

He nodded. "Stay close to the wall, though."

She began her climb. It was slow going, and she stopped altogether when she reached him.

"How you doing?" he asked, purposely making his tone light and calm.

She shrugged. And stared at him.

"Is there something you wanted to ask me?"

She nodded mutely.

"I'm all ears."

She waited some more. His mind raced through a dozen possible questions about divorces and new babies. Finally, she said, "You aren't Galaxy Man, are you?"

Ouch. "No, Debbi, I'm not."

"And you don't really live here, do you?"

"Not for keeps."

"Okay," she said.

"But that doesn't mean I don't love you."

She nodded slowly. "I'd better go get dressed." She walked past him, taking a long time to reach the top of the stairs.

Jarred watched until he couldn't see her anymore. When he turned to get back to work, he saw Beth standing at the bottom of the stairs, staring up at him.

He walked down to join her on the landing. "You okay?"

She shook her head. "Not really."

"Can I help?" he asked, slipping his palm to the small of her back.

She closed her eyes for a moment, then looked at him. The sorrow in her gaze made him ache for her. "I don't—" She stopped. Swallowed. "I don't think you should tell the kids that you love them."

He dropped his hand. "Right, sure."

She winced, and he went to touch her again, but she stepped aside. "I'd better go see about Caleb," she said, hurrying past him.

"Beth, wait."

But she didn't. She almost ran down the hallway to get away from him. He stood there, not understanding any part of what just happened. He'd hurt her, but he wasn't sure how. All he'd done was agree with her. She was right. Given the circumstances, it was better not to let the kids get too attached to him. So why had she run?

IT WAS ONLY NINE O'CLOCK when Beth went to her bedroom for the night. After a long and dreadful day, she needed the privacy and the silence. She needed to think.

She'd worked like a demon for hours. All afternoon. She'd pulled off all the wallpaper in the hall and the kitchen, layer after sticky layer, and she'd kept the kids busy helping her. She hadn't even sat down for lunch, choosing instead to grab a sandwich on the fly.

It wasn't until dinner that she'd had to face Jarred again, and by then, she'd gotten her emotions under control. He'd tried to ask her what was wrong, but she deflected his questions. He'd given up after a while, and the meal had been unnaturally quiet. Even the twins had been subdued.

After dinner, Jarred had tried once more. She'd told him nothing was wrong, and then she'd gone upstairs and played five games of Candyland with the girls while Caleb fought aliens on his Game Boy.

It was an odd, long evening, but it was finally over. All but the thinking. And the hurting.

She got undressed, then slipped on her ratty old striped pajamas. Washing her face took a tremendous amount of energy, and she actually paused to rest while she brushed her teeth.

It wasn't until she actually stood by her bed that she realized she couldn't get in. Not with those sheets. Not with his scent still in them.

Despite her fatigue, she stripped the bed and re-made it, piling the old sheets in the corner until tomorrow. Finally, she climbed in bed and gathered her pillow in her arms.

It shouldn't have hurt. Not like this, at least. She'd known all along that he wasn't here to stay. She was the one who'd instigated their lovemaking, not him. None of it was really his fault.

She remembered his story once more, and for the first time, she really understood what he had said. Subconsciously, she'd been just as guilty as the girls in making him a hero, come by some twist of kind fate to rescue them from the cold, cruel world. She'd made him Prince Charming without his permission. Just because they had a mutual attraction didn't mean they were meant for each other. He was nice, and considerate, and he didn't have any ulterior motives.

From the first day, he'd told her exactly what was what. It was her own wishful thinking that had led her down the path. Her own rose-colored glasses that had tinted the truth.

So if her heart hurt, it wasn't because Jarred had hurt her. It was because she'd been awakened from a lovely dream. A dream with a built-in happy ending.

Reality wasn't so tidy. She was on her own. The kids had to count on her completely. She didn't have a cushion of savings, she didn't have any marketable skills, and she wasn't very good at remodeling. That Jarred had come to help was the only gift that was true, and she was damn grateful for it. It was important to remember the favor wasn't for her, but for Sam, and not to make anything more of it.

Jarred had done nothing wrong. She'd just let her sense of romance get away from her, that's all.

She turned over to her other side and curled her legs up. The bed felt too big. Too empty.

Even if he did suddenly declare his undying love, she still wouldn't be able to make it work. All she had left in the world was this ranch. She wasn't about to leave it and become dependent on another man. Not even a man as decent as Jarred.

So the best thing to do was to let it go. To stop fantasizing about things that couldn't be. Get used to the big empty bed, the weight of her responsibilities. And let the carpenter be a carpenter.

CHAPTER EIGHTEEN

JARRED WOKE UP at the crack of dawn, amazed that he'd slept at all. His thoughts had run riot most of the night, filling his head with confusions and doubt. What he needed to do was get the job done and get out of here. Go back home where he understood things. Where he was safe.

What he wanted to do was another story altogether.

Somewhere between taking down that first wall and yesterday morning, he'd changed. Beth had changed him. What he didn't know was if the change was good or bad. If these feelings churning inside him were love or need or wishful thinking. If his desire for her was based on proximity or if it was something more.

That he'd entertained the thought of selling his business in Houston and moving here was enough to scare the hell out of him. He'd always been alone. He knew how to be alone. He'd had this vague notion of someday settling down, but it was a gray, hazy sort of notion. Not something to trouble his sleep.

The one thing he knew about himself was that he was a selfish man. He'd learned to be polite, but that was because he'd figured out that life was a lot easier that way. But every decision, every move, every plan he'd ever had was based on what he wanted. This whole thing, him being here and doing so much for

Beth and the kids, it wasn't for them. It was for him.
He'd never had an altruistic notion, he'd never gone
out of his way just to help someone in need.

So what the hell kind of husband would that make
him? How could he be a father to these kids? Just
because he loved Beth—if it was love—didn't mean
he was good for her.

He didn't know the answers, or even most of the
questions. He wasn't sure about anything except that
he wanted her. But wanting her didn't mean squat. It
was stealing the car all over again. Doing what he
wanted, regardless of the consequences.

Well, dammit, for once he was going to do something decent. Something that was good for this family,
even if it meant that he'd hurt for the rest of his life.
He'd finish the job and he'd go home. Leave Beth to
get on with the life she deserved.

Before he could change his mind, he went downstairs and got right on the phone. He called one of
his oldest friends, his mentor, Carlton Bishop. Jarred
gave him an abbreviated version of his situation, and
Bishop agreed to help. The plans were extravagant
and Jarred wanted things done faster than any job
he'd ever heard of, but with Bishop's help, and the
favors Jarred could call in, it was possible. *If* he could
get the manpower.

Bishop came through. No questions, no hesitation.
He knew the Fremonts, who owned the local construction company. He had resources in Casper for
paint, cabinets, furniture. Bishop made two confer-
ence calls with Jarred on the line, and by the time
they were finished, Jarred knew he could do it. It
meant calling in every last one of his personal favors,
but he got the labor, the materials, everything he'd

need at a price that was astounding. He'd end up paying damn close to what he'd originally figured for the job, but the house would be finished before he had a chance to screw things up with Beth even more.

Now came the tough part—telling her. She wasn't going to like his plans, or the chaos he was about to let loose on her home. But it was the best thing for everyone.

If it all worked out the way he figured, the ranch would be finished in a month, month and a half tops. Beth would be able to start inviting guests as soon as they were finished with the detail work.

In addition to the house, he'd contracted Fremont to rebuild the old barn and corral, which had been a fixture on the place for so long.

Luckily for Jarred, there were enough experienced workmen in the general area to have two shifts, so the construction would be nearly around the clock.

The last thing he did was book three rooms at the local motel for Beth and the kids, and he'd made arrangements with the Main Street Grill to feed them for the duration.

In a month or so, Jarred would have his debt paid to Sam. He'd be able to leave knowing Beth and the kids would be okay. He'd board the plane with a clear conscience, something he hadn't had in sixteen years.

But first, he had to tell Beth.

He practiced his approach as he went upstairs. Beth was in the girls' room, helping them change their sheets. At least she was when he'd gone down to make the phone calls. She'd told the kids they could stay home from school today after their upsetting weekend. He got to the top of the stairs and thought about turning around, but he forced himself to go on.

This was the right thing. It wasn't the way he wanted it, and it wasn't going to please Beth, at least in the short term, but it was right. He just had to keep that in mind when she read him the riot act.

Laughter met him at the twins' door. It sounded great. He'd missed it the last couple of days. Jeez, but kids were resilient. At least when they were six.

"Jarred!" Debbi cried, spotting him at the door. "We're making Mommy crazy. Want to help?"

He smiled with the irony of the little girl's question. "You bet," he said. "That's pretty much what I had in mind."

Beth had an armful of stuffed animals, which she was unsuccessfully trying to put up on pressboard shelves. He wanted her. It happened every time he saw her now. It didn't matter if she was dressed in her baggy overalls or in her birthday suit. She turned him on like a light switch.

"Is that so," she said, turning to scowl at him. "I think everyone should pick on someone else today. I'm crazy enough without the help."

Dammit, she was in a good mood. The pall that had hung over the house had lifted in the night, which should have been a good thing. It wasn't so great when he knew he was about to rock the boat again.

"Uh, Beth..."

"Uh, yes?" she said, her gentle mocking making this worse.

"You have a minute?"

"I think so."

"Want to take a little walk?"

She looked at him crookedly, trying, he was sure, to figure out what in the world he was up to. But she didn't press him. She just tossed the rest of the stuffed animals on the bed and said, "Stay."

The girls giggled as Beth met him at the doorway. She nodded for him to lead the way. He tried to walk at a steady pace, not wanting to rush things, but not wanting to make her think he was going to tell her something awful. The best thing he could do was just say it. Spit it out. Let her tell him exactly where he could go, then... Then punt.

They walked through the mess downstairs, the boxes, supplies, smells and tools that all combined into a home repair stew. Jarred pictured the place once it was finished. How warm and cozy it would be for the family, and what a great B and B it would make.

This was the right thing.

He let her out the front door and followed her, closing the door behind him. He didn't want the kids in on this until it was settled.

She went over to the side of the porch and leaned against the support beam. "Well?"

He smiled. "Okay, well, um, I, uh... Okay. I wanted you to know that I'm going to keep my promise to Sam and to you," he said, knowing he was starting out wrong, but not knowing how to do any better. "But I'm kinda changing the method."

The slightly amused look that had made her eyes shine turned to suspicion. "What does that mean?"

"I've hired two crews to come in, starting tomorrow. They're going to work two shifts. With the plans you have now, the work won't take long at all. A month, month and a half."

"I see," she said, way too calmly.

"And since the place is going to be all torn up,

with so many people working, I've made arrangements for you guys to stay at the Starlite motel until it's over.''

"Uh-huh," she said, keeping her gaze locked on his.

"And you don't have to worry about meals. I've taken care of that.''

This time she didn't say anything, but her right brow rose a notch.

"You can come out and watch the progress. That's no problem. We'll make sure it's exactly the way you want it. But you wouldn't get any rest here, so... If you get a job or something, the foreman over at Fremont Construction said he's got a real reliable baby-sitter.''

"It seems like you've thought of everything," she said.

When was she going to blow? It was like watching a pressure cooker on a hot flame. He couldn't read her at all. Couldn't anticipate where her arguments were going to come from. "I think so," he said, keeping himself as calm as possible even though he knew his pulse was racing. "I'll stay here until it's done. I'll check everything myself.''

She nodded twice. Very small movements. Just up, then down, up, down. It was coming, he thought. Any second now...

"How much is this going to cost?''

"Don't worry about the—''

"How much?''

"Only a little more than it would have if I'd done it alone.''

She quirked her head slightly. "How is that possible?''

He shrugged. "I'm in the business. I called in a few markers, that's all."

"I see," she said, studying him like he was a biology project.

He wondered what she was going to argue about first—that he'd made the plans without her or that he'd made the plans at all.

"Okay," she said.

"Excuse me?"

"I said okay. It's very generous of you. It'll be difficult, but it'll be over relatively quickly. I'll tell the kids." She took a step toward the door, then stopped. "Do you know what time the first crew is coming? Should we stay here tonight or go to the motel?"

He opened his mouth to answer her, but nothing came out. Her acceptance of his plan was the last thing he'd anticipated. Hell, it was just plain weird. "Are you all right?"

"Yes, why?"

"I just thought… I figured…"

"That I'd be angry at your presumption? That I'd resent you making decisions that affect me and my children without consulting me first?"

"Well, yeah."

She shook her head, sadly, he thought. "I'm all those things. But I'm also a realist. I know this is something you're determined to do. If it was just me, I'd fight you. But it's not. It's for my kids. What they need most of all is a home, and safety, and continuity. If this is what it's going to take to give them that, then I'm not going to argue."

"It won't be too bad, Beth. Inconvenient, but not

horrible. And then you'll have everything you need.
You'll be able to get on with your life."

"And you'll be able to go home," she said, so
matter-of-factly that he felt slapped.

"That's not why I'm doing this."

"Sure it is. And it's another reason I'm not arguing
with you."

"You really want me out of here, huh?"

She shook her head. "You've been wonderful,
Jarred. To the kids and to me. I'll never be able to
thank you adequately. But if you stay…"

He stepped toward her, not quite close enough to
touch her. But close enough to see all the shades of
green in her eyes. "If I stay?"

"It'll be very hard on the kids."

"What about you?"

She hesitated, then her gaze settled. "It's already
hard on me. You've been a great friend. An unex-
pected, generous, kind friend. I'll always be grateful
for everything you've done, and I'll miss you when
you're gone."

"Houston isn't on the moon, you know. There are
planes that go from here to there."

"Of course," she said in that same calm way that
wasn't like her. That didn't contain any part of the
fiery woman he'd grown to know so well. "We'll
visit from time to time. I know the children would
like that."

"Right," he said. "Sure."

She looked away for a moment, and then back, but
not right at him. "I'd better go help the kids start
packing. There'll be lots of laundry to do today."

"I'll take care of dinner tonight," he said, wanting

to take care of so much more. Wanting… He wasn't sure what. Not this. Not this calm acquiescence.

"Great, thanks." She stepped past him and into the house without a backward glance.

He didn't follow. Instead, he headed toward the field that had once housed a barn and a corral, the first place he'd ever ridden a horse.

There were relics of the old place still in the grass. A horseshoe, a faded piece of two-by-four. Before he left, there would be a new barn here to add to the atmosphere and give Beth some options about what she wanted to do with the land. But it wouldn't smell like Old Man Whittaker's barn.

God, all these years later and he remembered walking through the big gate for the first time. He'd kept his distance from the horses at Lost Springs. They always seemed big and terrifying to him. But when Sam brought him out here, taking him right out of school in the middle of the week, Jarred had slowly overcome his fear. Sam hadn't rushed him and neither had the horse. Barney, that was his name. The old roan was Barney.

He'd never thanked Sam for that day. As a kid, he'd been a real jerk. Always out for number one, hang the consequences. As a man? He wasn't much better. At least he hadn't been much better until Sam had brought him out to this place again. Until Sam had forced him to slow down. To listen. To respect those around him.

What he hoped, what he wished, was that some of the things he'd learned would take. That when all this was over, he'd leave Lightning Creek a better person. That he could go back to Houston and see things through Beth's kind eyes. That he'd have Sam's patience. That he'd laugh as freely as the twins. And please, God, that he'd finally gotten rid of the chip on his shoulder that he'd carried since the day his parents died.

Would Caleb take so long to realize it wasn't personal? That the answer wasn't to shut himself off from caring about anything or anyone? No, he wouldn't. Caleb had Beth. Every day. She'd pull him out of this, no question.

Look what she'd done for him, and he'd only known her a little more than a week.

This was the way it had to be.

Beth had her future to look forward to, and he had his past to clean up. The only thing was, he wasn't sure that the way things had to be was the way he wanted them to be.

He should never have come here. And he certainly shouldn't have kissed her.

As he looked at her land, at her home, he knew that leaving would be the hardest thing he'd ever done.

Damn that Sam Duncan.

BETH SAT ON THE EDGE of her bed, her nightgown next to her right hand, her hairbrush next to her left. If she fell asleep in the next ten minutes, she'd be able to get about five hours. But she didn't think that was very likely. Not with her mind racing like this.

Tonight was the last night she'd sleep under the same roof as Jarred. By tomorrow afternoon, the cozy illusions she'd created would be gone for good. Jarred would be a job supervisor, urging his crew to move faster and faster. His eye would always be on the clock, and on the goal of leaving her behind.

She'd help him. She'd do whatever it took to hasten the work, because tonight, as she'd packed the twins' bag with Galaxy Man comic books, she'd realized just how much trouble she was in.

She wasn't sure when it started. Maybe with that first kiss on the roof? Maybe when he'd made that first breakfast. It had grown through his kindness to Caleb. His attention to the girls. That turkey dinner.

And it had come to a head as he'd told her that silly bedtime story. That wonderful, heart-melting story.

When it had first occurred to her that she might actually be in love with the guy, she'd dismissed it. She'd chalked it up to vulnerability. Hormones. The need to be rescued. But as the day wore on and she examined her rationalizations, she'd come to realize that while all those things were true—she was vulnerable, he did churn up her hormones, and heaven only knew how much she needed to be rescued—they didn't make up the whole picture.

Jarred had opened a door in her heart. A door she'd closed years ago, when her illusions about Dan had come crashing down around her.

She'd been young then, and naive. She'd believed that she could change Dan if she tried. She'd believed that the children would make a difference. She'd believed there was something wrong with her.

Now she saw that she and Dan had never really been in love. There had been an early infatuation, mostly on her part. A desire to be happy and to build a family. She'd forgiven more than she should have in the effort to make her family strong. But Dan had never seen her. He certainly hadn't respected her. And after a while, she'd lost all her respect for him. No marriage could withstand that. No marriage should.

It was Jarred who'd shown her what could have been. His tenderness, his unbelievable thoughtfulness. She sighed, forcing herself to stand, to unbutton her overalls. To pull off her T-shirt.

Once she had her nightgown on, she headed for the bathroom. She pulled the brush through her hair, then turned on the water to wash her face. As she lathered her hands, it occurred to her that in all the years she'd been with Dan, he'd never remembered that she didn't like orange juice. It always surprised him when she reminded him, but the information never stuck.

The third day Jarred was here, he'd poured the kids their juice and filled her glass with cold water.

Just like that. After mentioning her preference once.

He always fixed her coffee perfectly. He offered to help with the cooking, the dishes, the laundry. He said thank-you. Not to mention his incredible generosity in bed.

She focused on washing her face, then brushing her teeth and putting on her night cream. When she finished, she turned off the light and headed back to bed.

It had been a mistake to make love with him. The one really big mistake she'd made through all this. Some things were better left unknown. It would have been easier if she'd thought making love with Jarred would have been like making love with Dan. She wouldn't have minded losing that.

But now she had that memory inside her. And not just in her mind. Her body remembered everything. Her skin had memorized his touch. His scent was so imprinted on her that she could find him in a sea of men if she were blind. His kiss had changed her lips forever.

If only…

She sighed, pulled back the covers and crawled into the cold dark space of her empty bed. As she clicked off the light, her gaze went to the window, to the shadow and light of the moon's glow.

If only…

She turned away from the window, away from her foolish dreams. He wasn't going to stay. He had a life in another state, a business, a history. A future. He didn't need the problems of a divorced mother of three. It wasn't going to happen, no matter how hard she wished for it.

She shouldn't have made love to him.

She shouldn't have laughed at his jokes. Or watched him play with Debbi and Karen. She'd been a fool to kiss him.

In time, she supposed, the memories would dim. She'd be so busy, she wouldn't have time to torture herself with thoughts of his stay. She had a business to grow, children to raise, a community to join. Perhaps, one day, she'd even meet someone nice. Someone who would want a life in Lightning Creek. Someone like Jarred.

At least he'd shown her what to look for. Kindness. Generosity. Laughter. Energy. Tenderness. Was there another man in Wyoming who had all those things? Was there another man in the world like him?

She adjusted her pillow, then did it again. But it wasn't any use. The comfort she was seeking couldn't be found in a pillow. It wasn't as if she thought he was perfect. He had flaws, just like everyone else. He was way too good at manipulating her, and he had that tendency to ask for forgiveness instead of permission. Those things didn't seem big now, but if he stayed, they could become an issue for her.

But then, she wasn't a paragon of virtue herself. No one was perfect. It didn't work that way. The best she could hope for was to find a man who tried. Who cared. Who took responsibility for his actions.

The problem was that she'd found that man. No matter how she tried to rationalize it, the fact was she'd fallen in love.

Fallen hard. Fallen for keeps.

Damn that Sam Duncan.

CHAPTER NINETEEN

"CALEB. *CALEB.*"

The boy looked up, and Jarred was shocked to see the old hurt back in his eyes. Dammit. He'd come so far. Since school had let out for the summer, he'd been such a great helper that Jarred had thought that he'd made peace with his situation. But looking at him right now, he knew it wasn't so.

"What?" Caleb asked, his voice filled with sullen anger.

"This is your room, buddy. You're gonna be living in it for a long time. You might as well help us make it someplace you like."

"So?"

"So, we're thinking about putting in a built-in desk here," Jarred said, walking over to the wall of the expanded attic. In the last three weeks, all the major structural work had been finished, including the new extensions up here. But he didn't want to add anything to Caleb's room without his input.

Caleb looked at the wall, then shrugged.

"What's going on, son?"

Caleb's face changed from placid disinterest to active fury. "I'm not your son."

"It was just a figure of speech. Nothing more."

"I gotta go," Caleb said, turning toward the stairs.

Jarred caught him by the arm. The boy struggled, but Jarred held him steady.

"Let me go."

"No. Not until you tell me what's going on."

"Nothing's going on. Leave me be!"

Jarred took hold of his other arm and faced him head on. "Look. You're not leaving until we get this settled. You can do this the hard way or the easy way. It doesn't make any difference to me."

"What do you want?" he cried, his eyes filling with tears.

"I want you to tell me why you're so upset."

Caleb turned his head away, but Jarred could see he was crying. "I can't," he whispered.

"That's where you're wrong," Jarred said, pulling him toward a pile of lumber so they could both sit down. "I'll tell you why. Because I know what it's like to lose a father. I know what it's like to have to move someplace strange. To have to be someplace you don't want to be."

Caleb still didn't look at him, but he'd stopped struggling. That was something.

"My parents were killed when I was your age. Both of them, dead in a car crash."

That got his attention. He looked at Jarred with red-rimmed, suspicious eyes.

"I swear to God. I was shipped off to live at the Lost Springs Ranch. Everything I'd ever known was gone. I was completely alone. I hated it. I hated it with every part of me. The food was strange. My bed smelled funny. The other kids were weird and mean. Every day was hell."

Caleb's tears had stopped flowing. But Jarred could still see the anger just under the surface.

"I made it worse than it had to be. A lot worse. I didn't listen to Sam. I fought him and the rest of the staff every way I could. But you know what? They weren't miserable. I was. They laughed and worked and enjoyed the days, while I stewed in my own anger and fear. I was the one who couldn't sleep at night. I was the one who felt so full of rage I knew I was going to explode."

Caleb swallowed. He didn't take his eyes off Jarred, though.

"So I understand how you're feeling about this. But here's the thing I didn't know. The thing that would have made all the difference. Caleb, nothing changed. All my anger, all my fear, all my crappy attitude did was hurt me. No one else. I still had to go to classes. I still had to do chores. But I missed out. I could have had a good time. I could have made friends. I could have slept, and laughed, and felt good about myself. I lost the battle because I was the only one fighting."

Caleb's brow furrowed as the struggle inside him fought its way to the surface. "It's not fair," he said, his voice as soft and vulnerable as a scared nine-year-old.

"No. It's not fair. But it's the way things are. So you have a choice. You can make the best of it. Or you can fight it each step of the way. Just remember, the only one who's going to lose the fight is you. Not your mom. Not your sisters. And not your dad. It doesn't mean they don't love you. It's just the way life is."

"But," Caleb said, blinking back fresh tears, "all I want is for things to be the way they used to be."

Jarred pulled him close and put his arms around

him, hugging him tightly. "We can't go back," he whispered. "No matter how much we want to. The only way we can go is forward. And the only way it's ever going to feel good again is if you surrender. Give in to the truth, Caleb. Make the most of what you have."

Caleb gripped the back of Jarred's shirt, and he cried. He cried for a long time, until he couldn't cry anymore. And still, Jarred held him. He didn't let him go.

The truth of it was that Jarred didn't want to let him go. Not now. Not ever. He cared about this mixed-up kid. More than that. He loved him.

THE MONTH WENT BY in a blur of activity. Beth was reasonably comfortable at the motel, and the kids were managing just fine. It turned out the manager had a little girl a year older than the twins who had an incredible Barbie collection. Caleb spent most of his time with Jarred. For the first time in months, her son seemed like his old self again. She wasn't at all sure why, although she knew it was Jarred's doing. He treated Caleb like a colleague instead of a little boy. Under his watchful eye, Caleb accomplished tasks she would have thought far too advanced.

But that was only a manifestation of the change inside. Caleb had turned a corner. He was happy. Busy. And the chip he'd worn on his shoulder had blown away.

Caleb wasn't the only one who blossomed under Jarred's tutelage. She learned how to use a table saw, how to mix mortar and lay bricks. She worked right alongside the men as she watched the old house transform into something beautiful.

One of the benefits of working so hard, such long hours, was her complete exhaustion at the end of the day. She didn't have the energy to feel sorry for herself. Even though her heart ached every time she saw Jarred, and every time they spoke, at least she didn't lie awake for hours, wishing for things that couldn't be.

He didn't make it easy. He watched out for her in a hundred ways. From checking if she'd had lunch, to convincing some friends from Houston to be her first paying guests.

What he didn't do was touch her. He always took the extra step or moved the final inch. One night, she dreamed about him touching the small of her back, the memory so acute it woke her.

He was nice, and thorough, and professional. She had nothing to complain about at all. Except, of course, for the small fact that she loved him, and he didn't love her in return.

JARRED SAW THE TRUCK coming down the road. It must be the painters coming out to start on the exterior. By the time they finished that, the floors and cabinets would be finished inside, and then they could begin the interior painting. After that, the wood floors would be repaired and polished, or new ones installed, and that would be that.

The barn was up already, and it looked enough like the old one to make Jarred happy. If Beth wanted to, she could bring in some horses or cows, and they'd have a fine home. She could also use the barn as a garage, which would help her during winter.

The pickup slowed to a stop in front of the big Fremont Construction truck, and Jarred saw it wasn't the painter. It was Sam. He'd been out here at least twice a week, always ready to lend a hand. But this time, the old man headed straight for the barn, and Jarred took off to meet him there. When he stepped inside, Sam was in one of the stalls, his gnarled hand running over the wood. "This was your idea," he said, "right?"

"Yeah."

"It's a good one. This ranch calls for a barn. It was empty without it."

"Beth doesn't know if she wants to raise any stock."

"She will. She'll want it for the children."

"I hope so," Jarred said.

Sam left the stall and walked slowly toward him. "Almost finished then, eh?"

"A few more days."

"Then what?"

Jarred shook his head. "Then I go home. I've been away so long, I probably don't even have a business anymore."

"Sure you do. They're doing fine without you."

"Thanks."

"You know I'm right."

"What are you getting at, Sam? Even you have to admit I've paid my debt. I'm finished here."

Sam nodded.

Jarred saw all his wrinkles and his white hair and the way age had dimmed his eyes, but he also saw the young man who'd brought him to this place so long ago. Who'd taught him so much.

"What's there for you, son?" Sam asked.

"Aside from the business?"

"Yeah. Aside from that."

Jarred stuck his hands in his pockets and studied the dirt floor. "I have friends."

"Friends," Sam echoed.

"And business associates."

"Aside from that."

"I have a house. A mortgage. A car. A satellite dish. A gym membership. A dry cleaner."

Sam shook his head again. "That ain't nothin' but nothin'."

"It's my life you're talking about, Sam."

"You have a house in Houston, but you've built a home here."

"I'm not staying, Sam. So just put that idea right back where you got it."

"Just 'cause you've finished the last coat of varnish doesn't mean you're not still needed here. That boy, he could use a man like you around."

"I'm not his father."

"But you could be."

Jarred freed his hands, although he probably shouldn't have. It would be too easy to throttle the old fellow. "Look, Sam. I understand why you sent me here. And I learned my lesson. I'm sorry I took that damn car, and I'm sorry that I let you down. But it's over now. I'm done paying my dues."

"I know that, son."

"Then what is it you want?"

"I want to make sure you're leaving 'cause it's what you want."

"Of course it is!"

"I'm not so sure."

"You don't know what you're talking about," he said, turning to leave. This conversation wasn't going anywhere.

"You love her, don't you?"

Jarred stopped. He didn't turn back, but he couldn't go on. His feet just refused to budge.

"You love her, son," Sam said again, only this time, it wasn't a question. "I've seen it in your eyes. Every time I come out here, it's worse than the last."

"I'm still the kid who stole that car, Sam, even after all this time. Even after paying you back, the facts don't change."

"That's where you're wrong."

Jarred faced his friend once more. "No. I'd like it to be different, but I'm a realist. I've built my life, my whole life, so that no one would ever have to rely on me, and so I wouldn't have to rely on them. I'll admit, I like Beth and I like her kids, but love... Love is too much responsibility for a man like me."

"If I believed that, I would have sent you home right after the auction," Sam said softly.

Jarred took a step toward him. "You didn't know if I'd stick around. Or if I'd stay to the end. Hell, Sam, *I* didn't know."

"I didn't, huh?"

"You hadn't seen me in sixteen years. The last time you laid eyes on me, I stole your car and took off without a backward glance. So no, you didn't know. You couldn't."

Sam smiled, the lines around his mouth deep from millions of smiles just like this one. "How do you think you got that invitation to come out to the auction?"

Jarred shrugged. "I'm an alumnus. Some secretary found my name."

Sam shook his head. "Son, I've been watching you

for years. Reading about your company. Asking some friends in Houston to keep an eye on you.''

''Friends? What friends?''

''Carlton Bishop.''

Jarred's head snapped back with surprise. ''Bishop? He's the man who approved my loan. The one who got me started. Hell, he made all this possible.''

Sam's smile broadened. ''That's the fella.''

''I don't get it. Why? Why did you care? I was a rotten kid, and I never did a good thing for you.''

''Tell me something, Jarred. Do you think Caleb is a rotten kid?''

He shook his head. ''Of course not. He's a great kid. He was just confused for a while. Afraid. But he's settling right in.''

''There you go.''

''But you had a hundred boys to watch out for. I wasn't anyone special.''

''Yes you were, son. You were special to me. And you're special to Beth and her children. It seems a shame to leave a place where people hold you in such esteem, just to go back to a gym and a dry cleaner.''

Jarred sighed. ''I don't know if I can do it, Sam. She's been disappointed before. She deserves so much.''

''You two deserve each other,'' Sam said. ''You think about that. And you think about what you'd be leaving behind. Do the right thing, Jarred. I know you can.''

BETH COULD HARDLY believe it. The house, her house, was finished. The paint hadn't quite dried, and there wasn't enough furniture, but it was done and it was real. Jarred had worked a miracle.

She ran her hand across the new kitchen countertop as she took in the beautiful workmanship on the cabinets. The brass hardware sparkled, and so did the china cups lined up in the new hutch.

It was far more wonderful than she'd ever imagined. Far more expensive, too. But she'd figured that out. She'd talked to Sam and he'd given her the costs. It was less than it would have cost anyone else in the world, but it was still a fortune. Of course, she couldn't start paying Jarred back for a while, not until she started bringing in some revenue. As soon as that happened, she'd pay in monthly installments until her debt, plus interest, was paid, even though it would probably take the rest of her life. It was far too generous to accept as a gift, no matter how well intended. Jarred would complain, but she'd make him see that she needed to pay him back.

She smiled as she heard the kids shouting upstairs. This was the first time they'd all seen the finished product, and they were more thrilled than she was, if that was possible. Jarred had gone to such trouble with their bedrooms. He'd remembered every detail, everything she'd told him, right down to the finishing touches.

He'd replaced Caleb's *Star Wars* posters with *X-Files* posters and had them framed and hung. He'd built in a computer desk and shelves, and even had a decorator from town coordinate the room in rustic browns and reds. The decorator had turned the girls' room into a sunny yellow wonderland, with built-in toy cabinets and canopy beds.

The sound of thundering hooves, or was it just

three pairs of sneakers, rumbled from the hallway as the children hurried down the stairs. She went out to meet them, excited to see their smiles.

"Mom! I can reach the hangers in the closet!" Debbi said breathlessly. "They're my size!"

"There's a table and chairs where we can draw and we can have parties and we can do our homework!" Karen hopped up and down in her enthusiasm, making her a little hard to understand.

"The computer is so cool, Mom," Caleb said, with more spirit than she'd seen in ages. "It's already loaded with programs. It has Myst and Doom and King's Quest."

Debbi started jumping with her sister.

"I love it, love it, love it!"

"Can we get a horse?" Caleb asked. "I'd take care of it. I promise. And we need a dog. This house needs a dog."

Beth wrapped her arms around Caleb and hugged him tight. "We'll see. Maybe, after I finish buying the furniture."

"Excellent!"

"Where's Jarred?" Karen asked. "Can we take him out to dinner, Mom?"

"That's a good idea," she said. "I think he's in the first guest room. Why don't you go knock on his door and ask him?"

The girls sprinted up the stairs. Caleb stayed with her, and he didn't even make her stop hugging him. If it weren't for one thing, this would surely be the happiest day of her life. But that one thing was mighty big.

Jarred was going home. First thing in the morning.

And Beth didn't know if she could stand it, it hurt so much.

"Does he have to leave?" Caleb asked softly.

She looked into her son's brown eyes, so surprisingly mature for a little guy. "Yeah, I think so."

"Can't you ask him to stay?"

"I don't want to make him feel bad about leaving. Not after all he's done."

"He won't mind you asking," Caleb said. "I know he won't."

She gave him a kiss on the tip of his nose. "I don't think so, champ. He's got a whole life waiting for him. We've borrowed him long enough."

Caleb nodded solemnly. "I don't understand why people have to leave all the time."

"I don't, either," she said. "It sucks, huh?"

He giggled. "Yeah, it sucks."

"What sucks?"

Beth looked up at Jarred's voice. He was on the stairs, with Debbi and Karen each holding a hand. Just looking at him made her chest get tight.

She let her arms drop from around Caleb as she tried to answer Jarred's question. But she couldn't seem to make her voice work.

Caleb looked at her, then at Jarred. "It sucks that you're leaving," he said.

"Yeah!" Debbi agreed.

Karen nodded. "It sucks!"

Jarred smiled, but it wasn't an easy grin. There was too much regret in it. "I know. I'm gonna miss you guys like crazy."

"Don't go, Jarred," Debbi begged, tugging on his hand.

"Don't go," Caleb said, his voice so serious Jarred had to hear the need behind it.

But Jarred wasn't looking at the children. He was looking at Beth. Staring at her as if he'd never seen her before. His brow was furrowed, and his head tilted slightly to the left.

"Hey, kids," she said. "Why don't you all go outside and look at the barn."

"We want to stay," Karen objected.

Caleb went over to her and held out his hand. "Come on, pip-squeak. Let's go."

"But, Caleb!"

He took her free hand and pulled, picking up Debbi on his way to the door. "You're so dense," he said. "Can't you see they want to be alone?"

The door shut behind them, and then it was just Jarred. Standing at the bottom of the stairs. Looking at her with those light-blue eyes.

"I want to tell you a story," she said.

He nodded, not moving. Not taking his eyes off her.

"It doesn't start once upon a time, though. It starts about a month ago, at a charity auction."

He took the last step down and started toward her, moving slowly in a straight line.

"At this auction," she said, "there was a very scared lady and her three kids. And she didn't know how she was going to start her new life. She was fairly shaking in her boots. But then she met a carpenter."

He was next to her now. At arm's length. Close enough for her to see the quandary in his gaze.

"And he came to her house and changed everything. He built her a castle, and he made her feel wanted, and he was the kindest, most generous carpenter in the whole world. The lady would never forget him. Not for the rest of her life.''

''I—''

Beth took in a steadying breath, then let it out slowly. ''And the lady wished he could stay forever.''

Jarred froze. He looked at her with an intensity that took her breath away. He looked inside her. Into the part of her she'd never shared before.

''You'd be taking a big risk,'' he whispered. ''I don't have a very good track record.''

''Records are made to be broken,'' she said.

''I've never tried 'forever' before.''

She smiled, the hope filling her so full she was about to burst. ''You only need to get it right once.''

Then she watched as he made up his mind. It was right there on his beautiful face. The decision was made. And it was good.

He slipped his arm around her, placing his palm on the small of her back. Pulling her toward him, into the safety of his arms. ''Beth,'' he whispered, the word so filled with love it was like a prayer. ''Beth, I love you. I don't want to go. I never want to leave here.''

''Oh, Jarred,'' she said with a sigh. ''Stay. Stay.''

His lips found hers, and she fell into his kiss.

She hardly heard her three itty-bitty children cheering on the front porch. He was a carpenter. And he was a hero. But best of all, he was family.

All for the bargain price of $4.98.

HEART OF THE WEST

continues with

IT HAPPENED ONE WEEKEND

by

Kristin Gabriel

When the bachelor Katie O'Hara bid on fair and square refused to take her with him to Montana for the weekend, she did what was necessary—stowed away in his trunk! Katie was convinced the key to her past lay at Adam's partner's remote Montana ranch, so if she had to spend several days in close quarters with a gorgeous, unattached, pretty spectacular man...well, a girl had to do what a girl had to do!

Here's a preview!

"WILL YOU MARRY ME?"

Katie looked up, startled by the deep voice of the man standing across the serving table. His blue eyes matched the wide Wyoming sky.

She took a deep breath. "What did you say?"

"I asked you to marry me." The stranger smiled at her, looking tall and cool and gorgeous. "Although I realize we haven't even been introduced yet. What's your name?"

She hesitated. "Katie. Katie O'Hara."

"I'm Adam Harper and this is my third helping of barbecue." He held up his plate. "They say the way to a man's heart is through his stomach and, lady, I'm in love."

She swallowed, unnerved by the sexy dimple in his right cheek. "I'll tell Ernie you said so."

"Who's Ernie?"

"The cook. He's not married either, so you may be in luck."

He frowned. "That puts a definite damper on my honeymoon fantasies. I pictured you and me and a big bottle of barbecue sauce."

She blushed, still not used to flirting with the customers. Marge was a pro at the waitress game and had the generous tips to prove it. But after six weeks on the job, Katie still couldn't handle a simple flirtation. So she fell back on one of her favorite lines from her favorite book. "You, sir, are no gentleman."

"While you, ma'am, are the prettiest lady here."

The statement was so ridiculous it made her laugh. "Which do you think does more for me, the apron or the hairnet?"

"Definitely the hairnet."

She patted her confined curls. "Well then, I may just have to rethink that marriage proposal after all."

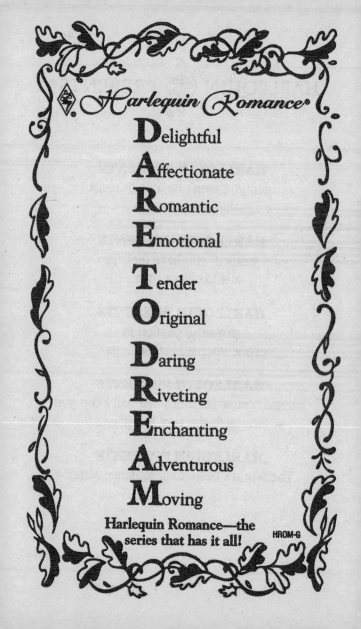

Harlequin Romance®

Delightful

Affectionate

Romantic

Emotional

Tender

Original

Daring

Riveting

Enchanting

Adventurous

Moving

Harlequin Romance—the
series that has it all!

HROM-G

HARLEQUIN PRESENTS®

HARLEQUIN PRESENTS
men you won't be able to resist
falling in love with...

HARLEQUIN PRESENTS
women who have feelings
just like your own...

HARLEQUIN PRESENTS
powerful passion in
exotic international settings...

HARLEQUIN PRESENTS
intense, dramatic stories that will keep you
turning to the very last page...

HARLEQUIN PRESENTS
The world's bestselling romance series!

Harlequin® Historical

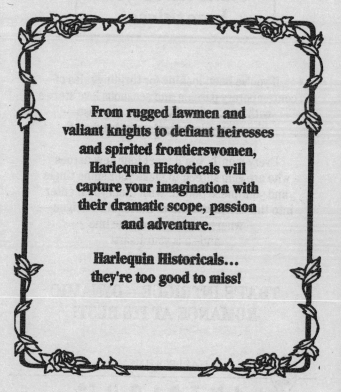

From rugged lawmen and
valiant knights to defiant heiresses
and spirited frontierswomen,
Harlequin Historicals will
capture your imagination with
their dramatic scope, passion
and adventure.

Harlequin Historicals...
they're too good to miss!

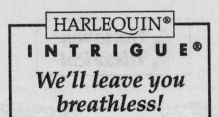

HARLEQUIN®

AMERICAN ◆ ROMANCE®

LOOK FOR OUR FOUR FABULOUS MEN!

Each month some of today's bestselling authors bring
four new fabulous men to Harlequin American Romance.
Whether they're rebel ranchers, millionaire power brokers
or sexy single dads, they're all gallant princes—and
they're all ready to sweep you into lighthearted fantasies
and contemporary fairy tales where anything is possible
and where all your dreams come true!

You don't even have to make a wish…
Harlequin American Romance will grant your every desire!

Look for Harlequin American Romance
wherever Harlequin books are sold!

HARLEQUIN SUPERROMANCE®

...there's more to the story!

Superromance. A *big* satisfying read about unforget-
table characters. Each month we offer
four very different stories that range from family
drama to adventure and mystery, from highly emo-
tional stories to romantic comedies—and
much more! Stories about people you'll
believe in and care about. Stories too
compelling to put down....

Our authors are among today's *best* romance writ-
ers. You'll find familiar names and
talented newcomers. Many of them are
award winners—and you'll see why!

If you want the biggest and best
in romance fiction, you'll get it
from Superromance!

Available wherever Harlequin books are sold.